CAMP CREEPY TIME

The Adventures of Einstein P. Fleet

GINA GERSHON AND DANN GERSHON

G. P. PUTNAM'S SONS

G. P. PUTNAM'S SONS
A division of Penguin Young Readers Group.
Published by The Penguin Group.
Penguin Group (USA) Inc., 375 Hudson Street, New York, NY 10014, U.S.A.
Penguin Group (Canada), 90 Eglinton Avenue East, Suite 700, Toronto, Ontario,
Canada M4P 2Y3 (a division of Pearson Penguin Canada Inc.).
Penguin Books Ltd, 80 Strand, London WC2R oRL, England.
Penguin Ireland, 25 St. Stephen's Green, Dublin 2, Ireland (a division of Penguin Books Ltd.).
Penguin Group (Australia), 250 Camberwell Road, Camberwell, Victoria 3124, Australia
(a division of Pearson Australia Group Pty Ltd).
Penguin Books India Pvt Ltd, 11 Community Centre, Panchsheel Park,
New Delhi - 110 017, India.
Penguin Group (NZ), Cnr Airborne and Rosedale Roads, Albany, Auckland 1310,
New Zealand (a division of Pearson New Zealand Ltd).
Penguin Books (South Africa) (Pty) Ltd, 24 Sturdee Avenue, Rosebank,
Johannesburg 2196, South Africa.
Penguin Books Ltd, Registered Offices: 80 Strand, London WC2R oRL, England.

Library of Congress Cataloging-in-Publication Data
Gershon, Gina. Camp Creepy Time / Gina Gershon and Dann Gershon.   p. cm.
Summary: Surrounded by monsters, befriended by a ghost, and having discovered
that Camp Creepy Time's counselors are aliens, thirteen-year-old Einstein P. Fleet's only
hope of help is Roxie, a girl who keeps appearing and disappearing with no explanation.
[1. Camps—Fiction. 2. Supernatural—Fiction. 3. Extraterrestrial beings—Fiction. 4. Humorous
stories.] I. Gershon, Dann. II. Title.   PZ7.G3182Cam 2007   [Fic]—dc22 2006020521

ISBN 978-0-399-24737-8
1 3 5 7 9 10 8 6 4 2
First Impression

In memory of our father and simpler times.
Werewolves and mummies and vampires! Oh, my!

CHAPTER 1

Day One — 7:30 A.M.

He could not imagine a worse way to spend the summer. It would begin with a torturous, three-hour excursion in a broken-down school bus to the middle of God-knows-where, surrounded on all sides by a tribe of screaming lunatics. If he survived the ride, the next eight weeks would be spent with the same group of misfits in the equivalent of a maximum-security prison. Days would consist of a strict diet of inedible meals, strenuous physical exercise, and "special activities" normally reserved for patients committed to mental institutions. Nights would pass without the comfort of a bed, sleeping outdoors and being eaten alive by an unspeakable assortment of blood-sucking insects. No Internet, no blogging, no e-mail, no cell phones, no video games, no iPods, no television. The rules were quite clear. The boy braced himself for what lay ahead. As the motor exploded to life, his fellow inmates burst into song. The first day of his eight-week sentence had officially just begun. He resigned himself to his fate and stepped into the vehicle.

Einstein P. Fleet was headed off to summer camp.

As Einstein's parents watched the bus door close behind their oversized son, a sense of relief washed over them.

"Well, he's off," Einstein's father announced, waving good-bye to the back end of the bus with a rolled-up brochure in his hand.

Norman Fleet opened the brochure and stared at the scenic picture on the front cover. Recently refurbished and under new management, the place was too good to be true. It looked more like a luxury resort than a sleepaway camp. Horseback riding, hiking, swimming, canoeing, and kayaking were just a few of the things that the camp had to offer, including a small lake, an Olympic-sized swimming pool, and a fully equipped arts and crafts center. The cabins were rustic but charming. The brochure boasted a gourmet chef and a menu that was enough to make one's mouth water. Leaving nothing to chance, the new owners had even built a state-of-the-art infirmary with a professional nurse on staff twenty-four hours a day, seven days a week. It just didn't get any better than this, Norman decided, especially with a special introductory offer of fifty bucks a week.

"Camp Creepy Time will never be the same." Einstein's mother giggled.

"That's for sure," Norman agreed.

Holding hands, they watched the yellow bus disappear into the distance, enjoying their first real time without the obligation of being a parent in thirteen years. Though neither of them was willing to admit it to the other, the break was long overdue. Einstein was not exactly a problem child, but he was no angel either. There was the time that he "accidentally" locked his art teacher in the supply cabinet and conveniently lost the key in order to determine the effects that solitary confinement had on the human psyche. She spent six hours in the closet before the fire department finally arrived and freed the poor woman. Then there was the time that Einstein invented a new type of super epoxy and glued half of his science class to their seats to demonstrate how it worked.

The fact was that these scientific and social experiments were not isolated incidents, but more of a daily routine. As a result, Einstein and his principal were on a first-name basis. And, after five years of dealing with their son's oddball antics, Mr. Hearst had suggested to the Fleets that the boy was in dire need of a change of scenery, preferably to another school district. Einstein, however, had reassured them that he was simply misunderstood and that they should not let the politically correct attitude of one public school bureaucrat sway their God-given right to raise their own child as they saw fit and in the location of their choice.

For the most part, however, Einstein spent endless hours locked away in his room, blogging with others on his computer about any number of conspiracy theories. He even had his own website—*The Smoking Peashooter*. The site had attracted a large number of visitors and a cultlike following. Einstein and his fellow bloggers discussed everything from corporate cover-ups to political plots.

The main problem with spending eight weeks at camp was that it meant spending eight weeks without a computer. Einstein had fruitlessly argued that summer camp could wait, but the conspiracies that plagued the world demanded constant monitoring. He had even questioned his parents' motivation for sending him away for the summer. Norman and Shirley countered that the world could survive for one summer without him and that this conspiracy was not up for debate. The boy did not speak to them for days.

"He really looked upset," Norman said to his wife, having second thoughts. "Do you think he'll ever forgive us?"

"We're sending him to summer camp, not to prison," Shirley replied, nudging her husband playfully. "Besides, a little fresh air and some exercise won't kill him."

"That's not how Einstein sees it."

"Don't you worry about Einstein," she said with authority. "That boy's gonna have the time of his life."

CHAPTER 2

Day One — 7:35 A.M.

Einstein stood at the front of the bus and shook his head in dismay. All of his fellow inmates were dressed up like classic monsters from old black-and-white horror flicks. A sea of mummies, vampires, and werewolves were wedged into their seats, singing camp songs and swaying in unison. Suddenly, the little monsters stopped singing and stared directly at Einstein.

The silence was deafening.

A familiar pit formed in the bottom of his belly, and he started to feel sick. Einstein briefly recalled a recurring dream in which he stood up in math class to answer a question only to discover that he wasn't wearing any pants. He quickly checked to make sure that he hadn't made the same mistake in real life. To his relief, Einstein's shorts were in place, his fly was up, and he had remembered to wear his underwear. It took a moment or two before he realized the real problem. Einstein was the only camper on the entire bus who wasn't wearing a costume. He had not been away from home for five minutes and he was already the official camp outcast.

"Where's your costume?" the surly bus driver demanded, as

if Einstein had committed a federal offense. "You're supposed to wear a costume."

"What on Earth for?" Einstein inquired.

Befuddled by the boy's response, the bus-driving troll pointed to a slogan on his T-shirt that read **HAVE A CREEPY DAY** in big block letters that were wrapped around a bright yellow smiley face symbol, except the face wasn't smiling. "The opening day ceremony? Didn't you get an orientation package?" he asked gruffly.

His father had given him the orientation package, but Einstein never bothered to read it. He had simply tossed it into the pile with the rest of his homework and promptly forgotten about it. The bus driver seemed upset, so Einstein decided to employ the same tactic that he used when one of his teachers asked him about an assignment that he had ignored. Einstein shrugged at the man and played dumb.

"You were supposed to dress up like your favorite monster. That's how we decide which cabin to assign you to for the summer."

"What does one thing have to do with the other?" Einstein asked.

The bus driver looked at Einstein and shook his head. "You filled out the questionnaire in the brochure, didn't you? Werewolves stay with werewolves, mummies stay with mummies, vampires stay with vampires, and so on and so forth. We want you to live in a cabin of your peers."

Einstein never saw a questionnaire, let alone filled one out, but he had a sneaking suspicion about who had—his father. No doubt the bargain-basement price tag of fifty bucks a week was worth spending a few minutes on the Internet to fill out the questionnaire and assure Einstein a seat on the bus. Obviously his father had decided to omit a few small details about Creepy Time, like the ridiculous dress code. He eyed the bus full of costumed campers and firmly clasped his head with both hands. "Somebody shoot me and put me out of my misery," he muttered.

Einstein noticed an odd look on the bus driver's face and decided that the man might actually be considering his request. Taking no chances, he quickly made his way down the aisle and squeezed his ample frame into a seat next to a pint-sized camper who was masquerading as a vampire.

"I vant to drink your blood," Vinnie the Vampire snarled, threatening Einstein with a fake set of fangs. The baby-faced vampire wore a starched white shirt under a long black cape. His jet-black hair was greased back and formed a tiny widow's peak at the top of his forehead. With his high-pitched voice, the boy reminded Einstein more of Eddie Munster than the legendary Count Dracula.

"You want to *suck* my blood," Einstein corrected, trying to be helpful. "Vampires don't drink, they suck."

"You're wrong!" Vinnie hissed. "Obviously you know nothing about vampires."

"Are you sure?"

"I'm positive," the boy said with authority. "I've seen every vampire movie that was ever made at least a hundred times. I'm an expert on the subject."

"If you say so," Einstein conceded. He offered the boy a Twinkie, hoping to smooth things over.

"No, thanks," the vampire replied, baring his plastic fangs at Einstein. "I don't eat sweets. They rot your teeth."

"Are you an expert on oral hygiene too?" Einstein asked.

"Sort of," Vinnie replied, eyeing the Twinkie with desire. "My dad is a dentist."

"Well, your dad isn't here, is he?" Einstein replied as he reached into his backpack and extracted a golden brown treat still freshly wrapped in cellophane. "Have one, my man. It's the Rolls-Royce of pastries."

The little vampire's eyes froze with fear, which was not the reaction that Einstein had expected. As best as he could recall, vampires were afraid of crucifixes and wooden stakes, not junk food. Either the boy was taking his role-playing a bit too far or he was too much of a wuss to disobey his daddy the dentist.

As it turned out, it wasn't the Twinkie that Vinnie was afraid of at all; it was the pack of snarling werewolves standing directly behind Einstein. They were dressed in plaid flannel shirts and gray cotton pants. They all wore the same variety of dime-store rubber wolf masks and rubber wolf feet, which made a flip-flopping sound as they slapped against the floor of the bus. Einstein wondered if they had called one another before the trip to coordinate their outfits.

"You're sitting in my seat, chubby," the leader of the pack said to Einstein, stripping him of the Twinkie. "Move it or die!"

It wasn't the sharp curvy claws that protruded from his rubber feet that made Billy Armstrong menacing. It was the foul stench. His feet smelled like moldy cheese. Perhaps it would go unnoticed if they were outside in the fresh air, but in the crowded bus the odor was unbearable. Einstein held his breath and prayed for divine intervention.

"Sit down," the bus driver screamed at the werewolves. "You'll have plenty of time to kill each other later."

"Count on it," the werewolf threatened, eyeballing Einstein.

Billy took a big bite out of the stolen Twinkie to emphasize the point, and then zinged the rest at an unsuspecting mummy who was sitting at the back of the bus, reading a vintage copy of *Famous Monsters of Filmdom Magazine* and minding his own business. Einstein watched the mummy wipe the goo from his eyes and slide down in his seat. The pack surrounded the boy and howled, then moved on to work on a vampire that was in a heated debate with a portly mummy about whether *Abbott and Costello Meet Frankenstein* should be considered a horror film or a comedy. Unfortunately, they did not notice the pack until it was too late. Billy grabbed a fistful of bandage and lifted the mummy out of his seat.

"Let's spin him until he pukes!" Billy shouted. He pulled hard on the thick strand of gauze and, as the bandages unraveled, the mummy began to twirl in circles. The harder Billy pulled, the faster the boy twirled, until he was spinning like a top.

Things continued like this for the next hour or so as the sprawl of the city disappeared and was replaced with the empty nothingness of the Mojave Desert. Einstein contemplated the odds of jumping from the moving bus and surviving the fall. Surely he would be better off taking his chances out in the desert despite the obvious dangers. If the fall didn't kill him, he had no doubt that the man-eating desert vermin would. Scorpions, snakes, lizards, and a wide variety of other creepy crawlers lived in this hostile terrain, including his least favorite creepy crawler of them all, the spider.

Einstein had never been fond of the insect species on the whole, but he was terrified of spiders. One had once crawled up his leg and taken residence in his underwear, never to be seen again. Einstein was convinced that it was nesting inside him, planning to hatch babies and eat him alive from the inside out. Actually, he had gotten the idea from an old B movie, but the concept was plausible. He had been terrified of the eight-legged freaks ever since. The mere thought of them made him shudder. He could feel their spindly little legs tap dancing across his body and began to squirm. As they sank their razor-sharp fangs deep into his shoulders, he screamed.

"Why aren't you, like, wearing a costume?" the spiders demanded.

It took a moment for Einstein to realize that it wasn't spiders speaking to him; it was the two girls in the row directly behind him. They were simultaneously digging their long, black, manicured nails into both of his shoulders.

"Do you mind?" he said indignantly.

The two girls giggled. Einstein's anger quickly subsided as he got a better look at them. They were hotties. He noticed that they were identical in every way, all the way down to their long flowing black robes and their conical black hats. Both had dark hair, hazel eyes, and slim figures that had blossomed nicely. Even their noses were perfect. Not only were they the only females on the bus, but they were the only ones other than himself who had opted to dress up as something other than a mummy, a vampire, or a werewolf. Einstein had never had much luck when it came to the opposite sex, but his thirteen-year-old hormones had recently kicked in, and the possibilities piqued his interest.

"I just got out of prison for armed robbery," Einstein confided to the twins. "Wearing a disguise will violate the terms of my parole."

"Oh yeah, you look like a total gangster," the girl on the right said. "What did you do, rob a piggy bank?"

Actually, Einstein had been nabbed once for shoplifting a carton of Twinkies from the supermarket, but it was more a case of forgetfulness than a deliberate act of larceny. The security guard had placed him in the janitor's office for a few hours while trying to locate his parents. Having no luck, the weary guard finally decided to release Einstein on his own recognizance rather than listen to any further threats of unlawful arrest and police brutality. He even let Einstein keep the Twinkies as long as he promised to take his business to the 7-Eleven up the block.

"We're the Whammy sisters," the girl on the left announced.

"I'm Willow and she's Wanda," the one on the right added. "We're, like, you know, witches."

"Pleased to meet you," Einstein said, recognizing the hometown accent. Though he normally found the Valley girl accent as offensive as curdled cottage cheese, at this point anything remotely within the realm of his normal day-to-day life was welcome. Besides that, the sisters were kind of cute, and who knew what could happen over eight long weeks with no parental supervision.

"Are you good witches or bad witches?" he asked flirtatiously.

Einstein regretted asking the question. Willow smiled at her sister and then cracked him on the head with her broomstick.

"Take a wild guess, doughboy," Willow cooed as she whacked him once more for good measure. Not to be outdone by her twin, Wanda poked him in the forehead with her magic wand, leaving a small, red welt.

Einstein slouched down in his seat to avoid any further contact with the witches of Woodland Hills, gently rubbing his skull. This was the story of his life. Neighborhood bullies and now a camp filled with monsters. For this type of abuse he didn't need to travel to the middle of the Mojave Desert, he could have stayed at home and gone to summer school. He closed his eyes and let out a soft moan. If the bus ride to Creepy Time was any indication of what he could expect for the next eight weeks, it was going to be a very long summer indeed.

CHAPTER 3

Day One — 10:57 A.M.

The first thing Einstein noticed as he stepped off the bus was the heat. It was well over a hundred degrees outside, but it felt hotter. A whole lot hotter. The July air was bone dry and it was difficult to breathe without scorching the inside of your nose. August would be more of the same, but worse. A whole lot worse. Einstein felt light-headed and woozy, wondering how much his delicate system could stand before it malfunctioned and shut down altogether. Sweat poured from his mop of curly brown hair like a leaky faucet, blurring his vision. He removed his glasses and wiped his brow with a beefy forearm.

"Einstein P. Fleet?"

It took Einstein a moment or two to realize that someone was speaking to him. He put on his glasses and looked down his nose at a rail-thin man wearing a starched white **CAMP CREEPY TIME—LOVE IT OR LEAVE IT** T-shirt that showed off his muscular arms to the best possible advantage. He swooped down on Einstein like a hungry hawk on a grasshopper, grinning from ear to ear and scaring Einstein half to death. The overly cheerful counselor slapped a name tag on the pocket of Einstein's sensible short-sleeved perma-wrinkle camp shirt and moved back a couple of paces to inspect his handiwork.

"Welcome to Camp Creepy Time, Fleet," he said, shaking Einstein's hand. "The name's Tommy Buckman, but everybody calls me Bucky."

The nickname suited the counselor to a tee. His front teeth hung over his bottom lip like two oversized Chiclets. He was half man, half beaver. Bucky pulled out his clipboard and scrolled down a list of names with his finger, stopping at Einstein.

"Looks like you'll be staying in Cabin C, my man. You're bunking with the werewolves." Bucky tugged on the collar of Einstein's camp shirt and made a clucking sound. "Say, what happened to your costume?"

"In the excitement of packing, I must have forgotten," Einstein lied. "If it's a dress code problem, I'd be happy to go home and get it."

"No need for that, Fleet. I'm sure we can dig up a spare costume somewhere." Bucky rubbed Einstein's belly and laughed. "Of course, we may have to have it altered."

Einstein watched as the other campers were given their bunk assignments and wondered how to go about applying for a transfer. Maybe the next group of kids to arrive would be slightly more normal.

"When does the next bus arrive?" he asked Bucky.

"Next bus?" The counselor shook his head and laughed. "There are no other buses. You thirty-six campers were all handpicked by our staff."

"Handpicked?" Einstein replied. "Based on what criteria?"

"Based on your interest and knowledge of werewolves, mummies, and vampires. You've been to a theme park before, haven't you?"

Einstein nodded.

"Well, this is what we call a theme camp," Bucky said proudly. Then he bent down and whispered in Einstein's ear, "If Creepy Time catches on, we plan to franchise."

The midday sun pounded down on Einstein like a jackhammer and he began to feel woozy. "Could I get some water, please?"

The counselor patted Einstein on the back and handed him the orientation packet. "Nothing like a summer in the Mojave Desert. It's a little hot this time of year, but you'll get used to it."

"I need water," Einstein repeated.

"This here," he said, unfolding a large piece of paper, "is a map of the camp and a list of all the activities. The times and locations are all in your kit."

"Water."

"The cafeteria is right over there," Bucky said, pointing to a crooked wooden shack that looked like a set from an old Western movie. In no way did the shack resemble the luxury hotel that had been featured on the cover of the brochure. "So is the main office."

"Where is the infirmary?" Einstein asked weakly.

"It's over there," Bucky said, pointing to his left.

The main building was surrounded by two or three smaller structures. The wooden planks were warped, rotting, and in dire need of a fresh coat of paint. Judging from the termite holes that riddled the walls, the buildings were long overdue for the services of a good exterminator. The doors were lopsided and hung loosely on their hinges. The only windows that were clean enough to see through were the ones that were broken. All things considered, Camp Creepy Time was a regular ghost town.

"I think I'm going to be sick," Einstein moaned. Suddenly, the world began to spin. The ghost town was spinning. The ground was spinning. Even the bucktoothed counselor was spinning. The next thing he knew, Einstein keeled over, landing facedown in the dirt.

"Here you go, camper," Bucky said, holding a canteen up to Einstein's lips and regulating the flow of water. "Everyone has a problem with dehydration the first few days. Like I said, you'll get used to it."

He reached into his pocket, extracted two little white tablets, and handed them to Einstein "A couple of salt tablets and you'll be good as new in no time."

Einstein eyed the little pills with suspicion, but was too ill to put up a fight. He popped them into his mouth and swallowed, washing them down with a big swig from Bucky's canteen. His stomach tightened and he instantly felt like he was going to explode. Einstein rolled over on his back like a beached whale, closed his eyes, and prepared to die.

An enormous woman dressed from head to toe in white towered over him, mercifully blocking out the sun. Einstein opened his eyes and looked up. "Are you an angel?" he asked, fearing the worst.

"I'm the camp nurse, dear," the woman replied.

Einstein squinted as he tried to make out the blurry letters on a black-and-white plastic name tag pinned to the chest of the woman's uniform. "Nurse Knockwurst?"

"My name is Norkhurst," she said, correcting him. "Nurse Norkhurst."

Einstein wiped the sweat off of his spectacles and looked again. "That's not what your name tag says," he replied.

"You think that I don't know my own name?" she growled.

Einstein managed to get to his feet and slowly staggered toward the oversized angel of mercy. She scowled at him as he stared at her name tag. The letters were blurry, but still spelled K-N-O-C-K-W-U-R-S-T. He looked up at the nurse and smiled. Given she was the size of a Mack truck and lacked anything that remotely resembled a bedside manner, Einstein decided not to press his luck. "I don't feel good," Einstein replied, rubbing his distended belly.

"Have another salt tablet," she barked. It was an order, not a suggestion.

Einstein shook his head. "I feel sick to my stomach," he moaned. Before he could utter another syllable, he became violently ill, projectile vomiting all over Bucky the bucktoothed counselor, the nurse, and everything else within spewing distance. He threw up all over his orientation packet, all over his luggage, and all over several other campers who were now running for their lives. Einstein dropped to his knees and gagged.

"What's up with him?" Bucky asked the nurse.

"He may be having a reaction to the salt tablets."

"That possible?" he asked.

"Only one way to be sure," she said as she ambled over to

Einstein. The nurse held out a salt tablet and motioned for him to take it. She assumed the worst was over, but she was wrong. Einstein placed one meaty paw over his mouth and waved her off with the other.

"Look out," one of the Creepy Timers screamed as he dove behind a dying cactus. "He's gonna puke again!" Just as the camper predicted, Mt. Einstein erupted once more.

The nurse managed to sidestep the onslaught and escape with the other campers, but Bucky was not as lucky. This time, Bucky's orange-and-gray mesh sneakers took the brunt of the blow. The counselor just stood there like a statue, staring at his feet, unable to speak or move. "I paid one hundred bucks for these shoes." Bucky sighed, staring at Einstein in disbelief.

"You paid a hundred dollars for a pair of sneakers? What a rip-off!" Einstein pinched the tip of his nose to keep from smelling his own vomit. In a few seconds, his stomach began to settle. "I feel a little better now," he announced.

"I'm so happy to hear it," Bucky growled, snapping out of his stupor. He glared at Einstein with genuine hatred and then softened it up a bit, the venom turning into sugary sarcasm. "Anything else you need? A gallon or two of mouthwash, perhaps? A few packs of Tums? How 'bout I just spray both of us down with a fire hose?"

"If it's not too much trouble," Einstein asked, gingerly clutching the blue bound notebook that was now completely splattered with puke, "can I get a new orientation packet?"

CHAPTER 4

Day One — 11:27 A.M.

Einstein held up the makeshift map that came with his new orientation packet and tried to decipher the directions. He had already walked by two other cabins, but his was nowhere to be found. Obviously, either the map was faulty or his two-month stint in the Cub Scouts had been a total waste of time. He crossed his fingers as the next wooden shack came into view and hoped for the best. Spotting a large metal C dangling from the door, he dragged himself and his suitcase up to the porch and walked inside.

"Now this *definitely* wasn't in the brochure," Einstein moaned.

The inside of the cabin was in no better shape than the outside. In fact, it was worse. There were twelve rickety cots in total, six on each side of the room. The wafer-thin, moth-eaten mattresses looked as if they had been rescued from a dump. Dark green mold covered one of the walls, filling the cabin with a musty odor. Dust balls the size of tumbleweeds were everywhere and the floors were caked in grime. It was the filthiest flea trap Einstein had ever seen in his life, but he didn't have much choice in the matter. He was stuck here for the next eight weeks, so he decided to make the best of it.

Einstein inspected a mattress for vermin, then placed it on the bunk that was located farthest away from the mold-covered wall. He tossed his sleeping bag on top and lay down slowly to see if it would support his weight. The mattress sagged to within a couple of inches of the floor but held. Rusted coils poked through the lumps in the mattress. It was like sleeping on a bed of nails.

"Home sweet home." Einstein sighed.

The good news was that he had the cabin to himself, at least for the time being. Einstein assumed that Billy and the rest of the thugs from C-Block were either lost or busy torturing some of the other Creepy Timers. Einstein decided it was best to use the time wisely. He found a loose board behind the head of his bunk and removed it with a bit of effort. After inspecting the area to make sure that it was free of vermin, he carefully tucked his summer's stash of Twinkies inside, making sure not to damage any of the precious pastries in the process. Einstein removed two of the tasty treats and secured the board firmly back in place, then placed the Twinkies inside the bottom of his sleeping bag for later consumption.

"Be prepared, Fleet, old boy," he said to himself, recalling the one and only phrase he learned at Cub Scouts before the troop's den mother had an unexpected nervous breakdown.

A loud creaking sound startled Einstein. He eyed the cabin to be sure that he was alone. When it came to safety and sweets, one could never be too careful. Seeing nothing, Einstein donned a fishing cap that he had fitted with a mosquito net and liberally doused himself with bug spray. It was one of many contraptions that Einstein had prepared in advance to survive his summer at boot camp. Practical yet stylish, the cap made a statement. Einstein started toward the door and, having a second thought, turned and retrieved one of the Twinkies from his sleeping bag. Be prepared.

Suddenly, a feeling of dread swept over Einstein. Someone or something was watching him. He scanned all of the nooks and crannies of the cabin for any sign of trouble. A shuffling sound from the far side of the cabin got his attention. Einstein positioned himself in a kung fu stance that he had learned playing Mortal Kombat and prepared to do battle with the unknown. Before he could strike out at the invisible intruder, the shuffling stopped and the cabin was again silent.

"Is anybody there?" Einstein whispered, positioning himself to defend his stash of Twinkies. "I must warn you, I went to ninja camp last summer."

A furry black golf ball with eight legs and large protruding fangs emerged from behind the cot. The creature stared at Einstein, daring the ninja master to make the first move.

"SPIDER ATTACK!" Einstein bolted out the door and ran for his life, screaming like a madman for someone to call an exterminator.

The tarantula watched the spectacle with mild interest and then continued on its way. As it scurried toward the door and the safety of the open desert, the hairy spider became aware of another presence in the cabin. It froze in its tracks, sensing danger.

The tarantula never knew what hit it.

CHAPTER 5

Day One — 1:23 P.M.

Big Al Mackey stood at the window and stared at Einstein, shaking his head in disgust. In his long years of military service, he had never seen such a slovenly display. The boy could not be more than thirteen or fourteen years old and yet he was already twenty or thirty pounds too heavy for his age. America had grown fat on a steady diet of junk food over the years, and its youth exemplified the condition. Big Al knew that a couple of weeks of hiking through the desert would slim the boy down, but this kid was in need of a total makeover. The boy's clothes looked as if they had been slept in, and the remains of something white and crusty formed a trail from his mouth down to the collar of his short-sleeved khaki camp shirt. An unruly mop of curly brown hair framed his pudgy face. A pair of thick black glasses with Coke bottles for lenses magnified his dark hazel eyes. All in all, the boy looked like an oversized nerd. He was sitting down at a picnic table, sweating profusely and trying to catch his breath. It was pitiful. Suddenly, the boy noticed Big Al staring at him through the window and did something that in Big Al's mind was unthinkable. He stared back and smiled.

"Hmmm. Fat, sloppy, and impudent," said Big Al to no one in particular. "Well, I got my eye on you, mister."

Einstein took a notebook out of his backpack and jotted something down as he continued to stare in the direction of Big Al. Big Al could see his eyes dart from the paper and back to the window. Shifty eyes. Beady eyes. The eyes of a real troublemaker.

"Don't you have something better to do than sit on your butt all day?" Big Al shouted at the boy. "This is a summer camp, chubby, not a library. Why don't you take a hike or something? The exercise will do you good."

Einstein sized up the man in the window. He looked to be in his late fifties with short gray hair that was styled in a military buzz cut. He was wearing a tight white T-shirt with the standard camp logo. A silver whistle dangled from his neck. His ramrod-straight posture hinted at a prior life, either in the military or as a fitness instructor. The man had a look of authority. Einstein knew the type well. All of them felt it was their right to impose their will on others. Some people needed to be told what to do and welcomed the direction. Einstein wasn't one of them. To him, an authority figure was just another type of bully. Maybe they didn't use physical violence to intimidate, but there was no difference between the two. A bully was a bully and Einstein despised them all.

"It's a bit hot for physical activity," he shouted back at Big Al, "but if you feel the need to hike through the desert, by all means don't let me stop you."

"Get moving, four-eyes," Big Al commanded, "or I'll roll you in honey and tie you to an anthill."

23

Einstein shot Big Al a final defiant glance and abruptly pulled down the mesh net on his cap. He turned his back to the man, then yanked his shorts down to his knees, bent over, and mooned him. Satisfied that he had made his point, Einstein pulled up his shorts and moseyed down the road in search of a more secluded location.

Big Al pondered the boy and how to best deal with the problem. His future was tied to this little venture, not to mention his entire life's savings. There was no way on Earth that he was going to allow anything, let alone an oddball like Einstein, stand in the way of completing his mission.

He turned to Bucky and pointed at the boy. "That's the Fleet kid, right?" he asked, the years of command clear in his tone. "The one without a costume?"

Bucky looked out the window and nodded. "He puked all over my brand-new Nikes," he said, pointing down at the splotches on his sneakers.

"Which cabin is he assigned to?"

"He's in Cabin C with the Armstrong kid and the rest of the werewolves."

Big Al turned around slowly and smiled. "A couple of days with that crew ought to put some hair on that chubby little chest."

"I don't know, boss. He doesn't look like werewolf material to me."

"Find him a costume," Big Al ordered, "and let's see."

CHAPTER 6

Day One — 2:22 P.M.

Einstein stared at the empty barn and couldn't believe his luck. The place was perfect. Abandoned and left to rot, it would provide him with a refuge away from the other campers and the prying eyes of camp management. Most of the red paint had peeled off long ago and what little was left looked like random splotches of dried blood. The wood walls, warped from age and exposure to the elements, appeared lopsided, like an old man sagging under the weight of time.

Einstein searched the perimeter of the barn for an entrance. He walked around until he found a small door. The handle was missing and the hinges were rusted shut. Einstein tried to pry the door open, but it wouldn't budge. It would call for another solution. The boy backed up about ten yards and took a deep breath.

"Ramming speed!" he screamed, charging like a bull.

The door collapsed upon impact and Einstein fell headfirst into the barn. He got up and dusted himself off, wondering if he should go any farther. The inside looked dark and scary. It might even be haunted or, worse, crawling with all sorts of bloodsucking spiders just waiting to hitch a ride in his shorts. He stood still for a moment or two, allowing his eyes to adjust to the darkness, before he mustered up the courage to continue.

"No guts, no glory," he whispered to himself.

The inside of the barn was eerily quiet. The support beams that held up the roof were rotted away and appeared to be unstable. Several planks were missing from the sides of the barn, allowing beams of sunlight through. Patches of tall weeds grew in the areas that the sun was able to reach. Dark green moss covered everywhere that it wasn't.

An old pickup truck was parked in the center of the cavernous space. There was an official-looking insignia on the side door. It had worn away with time, along with the words that used to circle it. Only one word remained that was still legible—it read **POSTAL**. The back of the truck was loaded with several dozen cases of painter's and electrician's tape. Considering the entire camp was in dire need of repair and a paint job, the large quantity of tape made sense. Still, Einstein thought it was odd. He decided to take a closer look and headed toward the truck. Einstein took a few steps forward, then stopped dead in his tracks as soon as he saw a diamond-shaped pattern of silky strands. The truck was covered in cobwebs, and where there were cobwebs, there were spiders. His eyes scanned the area for any sign of life as he backed away from the vehicle. Rather than risk a run-in with a horde of eight-legged man-eaters, Einstein turned tail and ran as fast as he could for the door.

Safely outside again, he looked for a place to sit down and catch his breath. He stumbled upon a picnic table and gratefully took a seat. As his breathing returned to normal, Einstein mulled over the events of the day. He couldn't put his finger on it, but everything about this place felt wrong. There was only one thing to do. He would explain the situation to his parents and request that his sentence be reduced to time served. Einstein knew it was an exercise in futility, but he reached into his pack and removed his notebook and a black felt-tipped pen. Einstein ripped out a page and starting writing.

Dear Mom and Dad,

HELP!!!!!!!!!!!!!
The bus ride to camp was worse than expected. Considering the fact that most of my fellow campers are one step removed from Neanderthals, I'm surprised that I survived the trip at all. Did you know that this is a theme camp for monsters? Thirty-six kids, including yours truly, were hand-picked to take part in this mad experiment based on their answers to the questionnaire. Congratulations, Dad! You passed the test with flying colors. I'm officially a werewolf.

The pictures in the brochure were grossly misleading, but I suppose you can't fault camp management for good marketing. Compared to Creepy Time, a maximum-security prison would be considered a five-star hotel. My lodgings are dismal. The cabin (if you consider a shanty a cabin) is crawling with bugs and snakes, most of which are poisonous and most likely man-eaters. The lake (if there ever was a lake) must have evaporated from the heat, along with the stable full of horses. The "Olympic-sized" swimming pool is more like a swimming hole, although the toxic green waste and algae it is filled with is a tad less inviting than the clear blue water pictured in the brochure. The long list of "activities" was also a lie, unless you consider vomiting, sweating, or building a birdhouse out of Popsicle sticks a boatload of fun.

Danger lurks everywhere and the odds of surviving eight weeks in this place are slim at best. I had my first run-in with upper management just hours after my arrival. (Actually, it was more of a staring contest than a run-in, but it was still unnerving.) The staredown was with none other than Big Al Mackey, the infamous warden here at Creepy Time. Although I drew first blood, the senile old geezer looks like he enjoys a good fight and will no doubt be gunning for a bit of payback.

I beg you to arrange for an early pardon. I will not hold you responsible. I will not bear a grudge. Clearly, the strain of parenthood has finally taken its toll and you no longer possess the mental capacity for rational thought. The long and short of it is simple. Please arrange for my immediate release while I'm still in one piece. The clock is ticking.

Sincerely Yours,
Einstein P. Fleet

P.S. In the event that I do not survive, please feel free to rent out my room.

Einstein reviewed the contents of the letter one last time to make sure that he had properly conveyed the seriousness of the situation in simple terms that even *his* parents would understand. Satisfied that he had made his point, he then folded the paper into three equal parts, placed it in an envelope, and prepared to lick the seal.

"FREEZE!"

Einstein did as ordered, leaving his tongue dangling in midlick. He raised his hands above his head and assumed the position.

"Don't shoot," Einstein shouted back. "I have a little over three dollars in cash and a Twinkie. You can have the cash."

"Turn around and put your hands down, kid. I'm not going to hurt you."

Einstein did as he was told and was relieved to see a fellow camper standing in front of him instead of a desert desperado. She was barely five feet tall but exuded the confidence of someone a lot bigger. Her long brown hair was streaked with blue and her green eyes sparkled in the sunlight. She was wearing faux-leopard-spotted pants, ankle-high Doc Marten boots, and cat glasses embedded with rhinestones. Part grandma, part grunge. The girl was thin but wiry, wearing a tight short-sleeved T-shirt that simply stated, **CAMP SUCKS**.

Einstein dropped his arms back down to his sides and sighed with relief.

"Trust me, kid," the girl snapped, snatching the envelope out of his hand. "You don't want to lick that envelope."

"Why not?" he inquired, surprised by her speed and agility. "The contents of this letter are of a private nature. A matter of national security, actually."

"I can sum it up for you in just one word."

Einstein thought she was joking at first, but from the expression on her face he knew she was serious.

"What's that?" Einstein asked.

"Germs."

"Germs?" Einstein repeated.

"That's right. Germs." The girl let the information sink in for a moment and then explained. "The slightest infection can kill you, especially in this environment. Why take chances? Who knows where that envelope has been? It was probably manufactured in some third-world country teeming with exotic diseases. Malaria, cholera, whooping cough, plague, and probably some stuff we haven't even heard of yet. You want to lick something like that, be my guest. Personally, I'd rather kiss a lizard on the lips."

"You have a point," Einstein agreed, impressed with her obvious intelligence and sensibility. "Nonetheless, the top-secret, confidential nature of the contents contained inside of this envelope requires that it be sealed and sealed tight. Do you have a suggested alternative to the standard licking procedure?"

The girl extracted a large wad of chewing gum from her mouth and wedged it to the flap of the envelope, sealing it shut.

"Nothing to it!" she said with confidence, tossing the envelope back to Einstein and extending her hand in friendship. "Roxie Rosenberg, at your service."

Einstein stared at the pink wad of chewing gum layered beneath the flap and chuckled out loud. There was nothing he found more appealing than a bit of good old-fashioned Yankee ingenuity and a large slice of common sense. Roxie Rosenberg undoubtedly possessed large quantities of both and was kind of cute to boot. She was odd and enchanting and full of life. Maybe camp wasn't going to be so bad after all.

"The name's Einstein," he announced. "Einstein P. Fleet, ward of the state."

"Einstein, huh? You some sort of brain?"

"I think the name speaks for itself," Einstein replied, hoping that she was impressed.

"How 'bout I just call you Fleet?"

"Why not?" Einstein agreed, shaking Roxie's hand. "My jungle name is far too hard to pronounce."

"What are you talking about?"

"A sad story," Einstein began, delighted to have her attention. "My real parents were killed during a hunting accident in Africa."

"You lived in Africa?"

"I was quite young at the time. Left to fend for myself in the jungle."

Roxie eyed him suspiciously.

"I'm afraid it's true," Einstein continued without missing a beat. "I was raised by a pack of wild mountain gorillas."

"Mountain gorillas?"

"Lived with them for over two years before I was rescued by Watusi hunters."

"Watusi hunters?"

"Spent the next three years living with the tribe. Quite an education, actually."

"So who are these people?" Roxie asked, pointing to the name and address written on the front of the envelope.

"The Fleets are missionaries. They bought me from the tribe for a handful of trinkets and brought me back to live with them in Encino."

"I see."

"It took years to get the jungle out of my veins, but eventually the missionaries tamed my heathen soul and I was fit to live amongst the civilized. The Fleets are simple, God-fearing people, the salt of the Earth. They sent me to this place so I would not forget the lessons I learned in the jungle and to hone my survival skills."

"That's the silliest thing I've ever heard," Roxie told Einstein, nudging him hard in the ribs.

Einstein smiled at her, but refused to retract his story.

"So, what's a bon vivant like you doing in a place like this?" Einstein asked her, deciding to change the subject. The jungle story had gotten him beaten up on many an occasion, but it did not deter him from telling it whenever the opportunity arose.

"I'm on a top-secret mission," she replied.

"What kind of mission?" Einstein asked, genuinely curious to know.

"I could tell you, but then I'd have to kill you," Roxie answered, sounding like she meant business.

"Which cabin are you in?" he asked.

Einstein did not recall seeing her on the bus, but then again, everyone was in costume. All of the others had remained in character despite the oppressive heat, reinforcing Einstein's opinion that most of the Creepy Timers were in need of serious therapy.

"That's on a need-to-know basis, Fleet."

"I need to know," he replied.

"No," she said firmly. "You don't."

Einstein enjoyed a good game of cat and mouse. So did Roxie, obviously. Getting information out of her was like trying to pry a clamshell open with a baseball card. He decided to try the warm and friendly approach to see if he could loosen her up a bit. Einstein pulled a crumpled piece of paper from his back pocket and showed it to her.

"I'm assigned to Cabin C."

"They put you in C-Block?"

"What's wrong with that?" Einstein asked, noticing the concern in her eyes.

"You're bunking with the werewolves."

"Don't remind me," Einstein moaned. "They're like a pack of wild hyenas. I'm not even sure if they're potty trained."

Roxie did not discuss the matter further, sensing it would only serve to upset Einstein. Instead, they sat together for a few minutes, quietly watching some nasty-looking wasps fight over the discarded remains of a half-eaten peanut butter and jelly sandwich.

"Speak of the devil," Einstein said, shaking his head in disgust.

Billy Armstrong and the rest of the gang were jogging down the dirt road, chasing a camper. The camper was dressed up as a mummy, which limited his movement, and his bandages were filled with brown stains. The werewolves were pelting the poor, helpless camper with dirt clods and cheering at every direct hit.

"What a bunch of jerks," Roxie said angrily. "We gotta do something."

Einstein picked up a medium-sized dirt clod, palmed it like a softball, and then pointed his index finger at the werewolves. Roxie got the drift of what Einstein had in mind and nodded her approval.

"It's all in the timing," Einstein said, sizing up an object about fifty feet away. "See that trash can over there?"

"The one with all the yellow-and-black-striped insects swarming around it?"

"They're called yellow jackets. It's kind of like a cross between a bee and a wasp, but these bad boys are a lot nastier."

"How so?" Roxie asked.

"A bee stings you once and then it dies. A yellow jacket bites and it doesn't. They can bite you five or ten times in a matter of seconds. Makes a bee sting seem like nothing."

Einstein could see by the look on her face that Roxie had put two and two together. He pointed at Billy and smiled. "I'll bet you a buck."

"You're on," Roxie replied.

Einstein let the clump of dirt fly, timing the throw perfectly.

It smashed into the trash can moments ahead of Billy and the other werewolves, thoroughly annoying the insects. The wolf pack screamed as the yellow-and-black swarm attacked. They were still screaming as they disappeared over the hill, with the yellow jackets in hot pursuit.

"Nice toss," Roxie said. She raised her hand and gave Einstein five. "There may be more to you than meets the eye, Fleet."

"Are you forgetting something?" Einstein asked. He turned his palm up and rubbed his thumb to his forefingers. "You owe me a buck. Fast pay makes fast friends."

Roxie reached into her pocket and smiled. "Don't have it," she said, turning her pockets inside out as proof. "But I'd rather owe it to you than cheat you out of it."

Einstein laughed. No doubt about it, the girl had style. He looked down at his wristwatch and noticed the time. "Are you going to the camp orientation?" Einstein inquired.

Orientation was scheduled for seven o'clock. It would be held right outside the main dining room, directly following dinner. If lunch was any sign of the meals to come, Einstein was going to be a lot thinner before the end of the summer, if he didn't die of malnutrition first.

"What for? Orientation is for weenies."

They exchanged conspiratorial looks and smiled. The girl was unlike anyone Einstein had ever met before. Most people would have walked away shaking their heads once they heard the bit about the mountain gorillas. Roxie seemed amused. He dug into his backpack and fished out two golden treats.

"Could I interest you in a Twinkie, comrade?"

CHAPTER 7

Day One — 6:08 P.M.

Dinner at Camp Creepy Time was served promptly at six and ended an hour later. No exceptions and no excuses. Rows of dingy green picnic tables were crammed into a stark auditorium that served both as a dining room and a gathering place for indoor activities, although the only activities appeared to be eating three mediocre meals a day. The memory of lunch was still etched in Einstein's mind and would most likely haunt him for the rest of his days. The thought of eight weeks of eating hog slop was not very appealing, but what was the alternative?

The food was not the only problem with the cafeteria. Lacking ventilation, fans, or anything else that remotely resembled air-conditioning, the temperature in the cramped auditorium was easily twenty degrees hotter than it was outside—and the temperature outside was an inferno. At least three or four campers had passed out from dehydration during lunch and several more already seemed to be reeling from the heat. A big bowl of salt tablets was strategically placed in the center of the buffet for easy access. The tablets prevented dehydration and, given the quality of the camp cuisine, were as edible as anything else on the menu.

The camp cook was nicknamed Curly. Considering he barely had a hair on his head, the name didn't quite fit. He was short and squat, with big, bushy eyebrows and a perpetual smirk that gave one the impression that the guy was up to no good. Clad in a gravy-stained white apron and a bright blue baseball cap, the sweaty little man personally supervised the buffet line. Einstein recognized him from the bus ride, although Einstein had spent most of the time looking at the back of his balding head. Curly doubled as both the camp cook and the bus driver. The fact that the man could not cook or drive did not seem to stop him from performing either duty. Einstein noticed that Curly's socks were mismatched, along with everything else he was wearing. The man was either color-blind or a hopeless slob.

"Don't forget to take your salt tablets," Curly the Cook bellowed as he ladled a mound of purple mush that vaguely resembled Jell-O onto the plate of a somewhat weary camper.

"What's this wilted green stuff?" the next camper asked.

"It's lettuce," Curly answered, eyeing the boy down. "Haven't you ever seen lettuce before?"

The camper took a second look at the green pile of moss and scratched his head.

Before the boy could answer, Curly shouted, "NEXT!"

Einstein slid his empty tray across the rusted silver bars and up to the front of the line.

"What can I do you for?" Curly asked, noticing the empty tray.

"You got any Twinkies?"

"You see any Twinkies?" the cook replied sarcastically.

"How about a slice of cheese pizza?" Einstein asked hopefully. Sweets and pizza constituted the bulk of his diet. In fact, it was all that he would eat. His parents had pleaded with him to expand his menu and eat healthier, but everything else that he tried made him sick to his stomach.

"What you see is what I got, little man," Curly said, distracted by a big black horsefly circling his head. With a sudden, unexpected motion the cook sprang into action, catching the fly in midair. He paused for a brief second to pull off its wings, then popped it in his mouth and began to chew without giving the matter a second thought. "Try some white bread with ketchup and a slice of American cheese. It's the same thing."

"No, thanks," Einstein replied as he watched the cook wolf down the horsefly. "I seem to have lost my appetite."

"Suit yourself," Curly the Cook said. Without missing a beat, he turned his attention to his next victim. "What can I do you for, camper?"

Einstein stared down at his empty tray and listened to the sound of his stomach growling. He was starving. The food was truly inedible and he was running out of Twinkies. There was no doubt about it. He was going to die of starvation. Einstein watched Bucky and Nurse Knockwurst piling logs into the fire pit outside in preparation for the orientation meeting. They doused the logs with gasoline and tossed in a match. The flames leapt from the pit like a Viking funeral pyre. Einstein briefly considered tossing himself into the pit to end his suffering, but then had a better idea.

"Will they be roasting marshmallows at orientation?" he asked the cook.

Curly pulled a large bag of fluffy white balls from beneath the serving table and shook it. "All you can eat, kid."

Einstein drooled at the thought of marshmallows roasting over an open fire. If camp management planned to serve something edible for a change, he wanted to make sure that he got to the campfire ahead of the rest of the starving campers, armed with a long, sharp stick and a good seat next to the fire. Orientation may be for weenies, but even a weenie needed to eat. He dropped the tray in a pile of other unused trays and headed for the door.

"See you around the campfire, Curly."

CHAPTER

8

Day One — 7:10 P.M.

The campers gathered around the pit waited impatiently for Curly to show up with the marshmallows. Some of them were shaking their sticks at Bucky and Nurse Knockwurst; others had engaged in sword fights as they jockeyed for position next to the roaring fire. Einstein had moved to a safe position behind the ruckus, wisely choosing to steer clear of the angry mob.

"What's the holdup?" one camper screamed.

"What about the marshmallows?" another camper shouted.

Einstein noticed that most of the campers were still wearing their costumes, but a few had abandoned them in favor of T-shirts and shorts. Everyone seemed tired and irritable. Considering the heat factor and the lack of a decent meal since they arrived, Einstein thought it was understandable. He looked around for Roxie, but she was nowhere to be found. Oddly enough, she wasn't the only one who was missing from the camp orientation. The scuttlebutt going around the campfire was that some of the campers had decided to go over the wall.

Einstein figured that the no-shows were probably still sick from lunch. He found it hard to believe that anyone would be crazy enough to try to walk across the desert, considering the obstacles. Nonetheless, desperate situations called for desperate measures and, judging by the angry mob, anything was possible.

"Let's get this show on the road!" a camper roared.

Before the ruckus could turn into a full-blown riot, Curly and Big Al arrived, each loaded down with several bags of marshmallows. The starving campers started to rush them, but Nurse Knockwurst put her foot down, literally stepping on the back of one poor soul and pinning him face-first into the dirt.

"Settle down and shut your piehole!" she ordered the camper.

The kids moved back and did as they were told, not wanting to suffer the same fate. Einstein took a seat at the back of the group and watched the camper grimace in pain. If this was Nurse Knockwurst's idea of getting them oriented to life at Camp Creepy Time, Einstein decided that he would make sure to stay clear of the woman at all costs.

"You want a marshmallow or not?" she threatened.

Fortunately for the camper, Big Al motioned for her to let him go. The nurse reluctantly removed her boot from his back and watched the boy crawl across the pit to join the other campers. With some difficulty, he stood up and took a seat.

"Welcome to Camp Creepy Time," Big Al started. "We are very happy to have you here with us for the summer and will do everything to make your experience at camp a memorable one. I notice that some of you have decided not to wear your costumes. Let me remind you that is against the rules."

"It's too hot!" a T-shirt-clad camper shouted. Several others nodded in agreement.

Bucky walked over and got nose to nose with the boy, like a drill sergeant working over a new recruit. "Do we have a problem, camper?"

The boy was too scared to move.

"Hot or not, you will wear your costumes or suffer the consequences," Big Al shouted back, staring at the camper. "Are we clear on that issue?"

The camper nodded and Bucky backed down. Big Al then continued with his welcome speech. "Many of you have brought it to our attention that the camp is not quite what you expected, but you have to appreciate what facilities we do have to offer and take full advantage of them."

"This place is, like, a total dump!" one of the Whammy sisters shouted at Big Al.

Before he could continue, several angry campers barraged him with questions regarding the list of "facilities" promised in the brochure.

"What happened to the Olympic-sized pool and the lake?"

"What about the stable?" another camper asked. "It's hard to go horseback riding without a horse!"

One camper made the mistake of actually calling Big Al a crook and demanded to be sent home immediately. Einstein watched in horror as Big Al lifted him off his feet with one hand and then slowly walked toward the pit. For a brief moment it appeared that Big Al was planning to roast something other than just marshmallows over the campfire.

"Anyone else think I'm a crook?" Big Al asked the group.

No one said a word.

"Anyone else want to go home?" he shouted.

All of the campers shook their heads in unison.

"That settles that," Big Al said cheerfully. "Let's all have a good time!" He put the camper down and handed him a bag of marshmallows, then playfully mussed up the boy's hair. "Just having some fun with you, sport."

The boy ripped open the bag and stuffed a marshmallow onto his stick as the other campers descended upon him from all sides. Big Al signaled to Curly and Bucky to distribute the rest of the marshmallows before the mob tore the boy apart. They tossed several bags into the crowd and watched with amusement as the campers fought over them. The scene reminded Einstein of feeding time at the zoo. As hungry as he was, he had no desire to get in the middle of this one. He turned to leave and walked smack into Big Al.

"Where are you going, camper?"

"It's a nice night," Einstein replied. "I thought I'd go for a walk in the desert and commune with Mother Nature."

Big Al took a marshmallow from the bag and impaled it on Einstein's stick.

"Nothing out there but rattlesnakes and coyotes, son," he said. "I'd stay close to the fire and toast a few marshmallows if I were you."

It was more of an order than a request, so Einstein did as he was told. He placed the marshmallow near the roaring fire and watched it begin to turn a lovely shade of Twinkie brown.

After a while, the skin began to bubble and caught fire, turning the light brown skin into a crusty black husk. Einstein removed it from the fire and blew until the fire subsided and the gooey treat was cool enough to eat. He took a large bite without even bothering to remove it from the stick and spit it out. "This marshmallow tastes like salt!" Einstein shouted.

"I don't see anyone else complaining," Big Al told him.

"I'm allergic to salt," Einstein replied.

"No one is allergic to salt," Big Al growled. "Stop whining and start eating."

"Are you deaf? I told you that my system is salt intolerant." Einstein stuck the marshmallow back in the fire and defiantly watched it burn.

Big Al walked toward him with menace in his eyes. "And I told you to eat it, you little twerp!"

"You eat it!" Einstein shouted. He pulled the flaming marshmallow from the fire, bent his stick back, and flung it at Big Al. The fiery orb soared over his head and landed with a splat in the middle of Bucky's back. The counselor howled in pain as he rolled in the dirt and attempted to extinguish the flames.

"Marshmallow fight!" one of the campers shouted.

The angry campers used their sticks like catapults and filled the sky with flaming marshmallows. Einstein watched with satisfaction as Big Al and the rest of the counselors ran for cover. Orientation had turned out to be a lot more fun than he had expected, even if he was still starving and surrounded by a bunch of lunatics dressed up as make-believe monsters. Maybe he'd get lucky and they'd burn down the camp. He'd wake up in the morning, discover the camp had been reduced to ashes, and go home. Einstein realized that it was just wishful thinking, but he believed that it was important to always maintain a positive attitude. With that in mind, he leisurely strolled back to his cabin for a Twinkie and a good night's sleep.

CHAPTER

9

Day One — 9:16 P.M.

Dear Mom and Dad,

Help!!!!!!!!!!
I survived my first day at Creepy Time, but who knows how long I can hold out under these conditions. The food is putrid, the kitchen is filthy, and Curly the Cook looks like the poster boy for dysentery. No doubt I will have to ration my supply of Twinkies if I have any hope of surviving the summer.

The mindless thugs with whom I share lodging in C-Block (lucky me) already have quite the Creepy Time rep. They've pummeled at least twenty campers that I know of and would have added a few more notches to their belts if they hadn't gotten the runs after lunch. I suspect that my fellow werewolves are part of some silly government program that allows juvenile offenders to spend their summer at camp as opposed to spending the summer at reform school (although the difference in this case is marginal). Billy Armstrong, the leader of the pack, is by far the worst of the lot. Not only is the boy in need of years of psychiatric therapy, he could use a lifetime supply of foot spray and a good bath. Normally, I'd welcome the opportunity to study a primitive primate species in their natural habitat, but I'd prefer not to be locked in the same cage with them during feeding time. My request to camp management for a transfer to a new cabin fell on deaf ears. My best bet is to lie low and hope that you come to your senses before it's too late or my roommates finally kill me and put me out of my misery.

Sincerely,
Einstein P. Fleet

Einstein tucked the letter in his backpack for safekeeping, clicked off his penlight, and rolled over to go to sleep. As his eyes began to close, he spied something moving out of the corner of his eye and sat up to investigate. Einstein turned the light back on and pointed it at the ground surrounding his bunk. Fearing that the spider had returned to attempt a night raid, Einstein had prepared to make a run for it when he was overpowered by the smell of stale cheese. The odor was nauseating, but somehow very familiar. Einstein held his breath as he tried to recall where he had encountered it before. Suddenly it dawned on him.

"Please, God," Einstein muttered under his breath. "Anything but this."

"Whatcha doin', nerd?" It was Billy Armstrong, up close and personal, occupying the bunk beside him. Einstein had gone to great lengths to make sure that he was as far away from the boy as possible, but apparently the plan had gone awry.

"Weren't you sleeping in the west wing of the cabin?" Einstein asked sweetly. "It's got the only window and a terrific view of the desert."

"Big deal," Billy growled. "Nothing special about a white ball in the sky and an oversized sandbox. My cot didn't have a mattress, so I decided to swap with one of the guys." The unfortunate werewolf whose cot was confiscated was now sleeping on the floor, or at least trying to do so. The moon was full and the light was shining through the window, directly in the poor camper's eyes. Billy looked at the boy and laughed. "How's the new cot, Norton?"

"This can't be happening," Einstein mumbled to himself.

"What did you say?" Billy roared.

"Don't mind me," Einstein replied. "I talk to myself all the time. Sometimes I even talk in my sleep. I scream when I have nightmares, which I have every night, by the way. Since we'll be bunking together, it's only fair that I warn you. I also snore really loud. Did I mention that already? If you want to move back to the other side of the cabin, I won't be offended."

"Shut your yap or I'll shut it for you." Billy glared at him for a moment to make sure that Einstein got the point, and then shut his eyes.

It was the first time that Einstein had ever seen Billy with-

48

out his werewolf mask on, and it wasn't a pretty sight. Just shy of six feet, the thirteen-year-old boy was tall for his age. Despite being thin and wiry, Billy was tough as nails and mean as a rattlesnake. He had fire-red hair and a blotchy red face that was an even mix of freckles and raw patches of acne. The worst thing about Billy, however, was his total disregard for his own personal hygiene. He had perpetually bad breath and body odor so foul that it was hard to believe the boy was actually human. Einstein noticed that Billy's feet were covered with tufts of thick, matted hair that surrounded yellow, crud-encrusted toenails of various size and length. Without socks and shoes, the stench was unbearable. Einstein made a mental note to purchase several hanging deodorant sticks at the camp store the next day. More than likely the camp didn't have a store, but he needed to keep a positive attitude. It was dark, but Einstein thought there was something very odd about Billy's teeth. They looked more like fangs. Curious, Einstein clicked back on his penlight to take a closer look. He realized his mistake instantly.

"Hey, get the light out of my eyes, you knucklehead!" Billy loudly complained. "You lookin' for trouble?"

All of the inmates from C-Block were now up and about and had gathered around Einstein's cot like sharks in a feeding frenzy. The whites of their eyes glowed with anticipation. Einstein thought it must be his imagination, but the campers all seemed to be getting hairier. He wondered if role-playing could cause such a reaction, especially within a close-knit group of psychopaths who had little or no grasp on reality.

"Hi, guys," Einstein said, doing his best to sound cheer-

49

ful. "Some night we're having, huh? Nothing like a good old-fashioned marshmallow fight to cap off a day of torture and mayhem. Is it great to be a werewolf or what? Hey, who wants to go outside and howl at the moon?"

The boys descended upon Einstein before he could say another word and zip-locked him inside his own sleeping bag. It was dark, cramped, and uncomfortable, but at least he couldn't smell the stench from Billy's feet. All in all, it was worth the trade-off.

"Thanks, guys," Einstein shouted, muffled by the cotton padding. "If I don't die of suffocation by tomorrow morning, let's do breakfast."

CHAPTER 10

Day Two — 8:19 A.M.

Einstein awoke to the roar of his own stomach, still trapped in the sleeping bag and starving. He suddenly remembered the emergency Twinkie that he had stashed inside and groped around until he heard the familiar crackle of cellophane. Einstein ripped off the wrapper and ate half of the Twinkie in a single bite. He considered eating the rest, but decided to be prudent about his situation. There was no way to determine how long he would be trapped inside the cotton coffin, especially since Billy and the rest of the werewolves were the only ones who knew where he was and they had put him there in the first place. If he was going to escape, he would have to do it on his own. Einstein took a deep breath to settle his nerves and concentrated on the problem at hand. It was impossible to tell if it was day or night. It was hot and difficult to breathe. From the heat, Einstein assumed that it was daytime. From the silence, Einstein assumed that the barbarian horde had left for the day, off looking for other innocents to torture.

"Hello," Einstein cooed sweetly. "Anybody home?"

Relieved to hear no response, Einstein let out a deep breath and began to work the zipper of his sleeping bag, praying that he could open it from the inside. After two or three minutes of grunting and squirming, he was sweating like a pig and beginning to panic. He applied two shaky fingers to a thick vein in his neck to check his racing pulse. Einstein was certain that he was moments away from a complete shutdown of his already overtaxed system.

"Need some help, sonny?" a voice asked.

Einstein froze solid and considered the possibilities. He could stay where he was and starve to death, if the heat didn't get him first, or leave the relative safety of his sleeping bag to deal with forces unknown. He was still considering his options when the zipper unzipped and blinding light flooded in.

He squinted a few times until the room came into focus. An old man was hunched over him, his leathery skin parched and weathered. He had long, straggly white hair that was tied back in pigtails and an equally straggly white beard. Einstein noticed that his hands were shaking and that he was a bit unsteady on his feet.

"You okay, boy?" he asked. The voice was as weathered as his skin.

"I'm fine," Einstein replied. "Just a little magic trick gone awry."

"I see," the old coot mumbled. "Not exactly Harry Houdini, are you, sonny?"

"Einstein P. Fleet," he said, holding out his hand, "leader of the resistance movement."

"You don't say," he replied, smiling at Einstein. "Ralph Waldo Greeley, underpaid and unappreciated mailman, at your service." He cackled at his own joke.

Einstein noticed that he had a tattoo of a rattlesnake coiled around a letter opener on his left forearm. The inscription at the bottom read **FIRST CLASS**. He was dressed in work boots, tattered jeans, and a tie-dyed T-shirt that was glued to his bony frame. Greeley looked more like an old hippie than a mailman. Einstein thought about the pickup truck that he'd stumbled across in the barn and realized that it must have belonged to Greeley. It must have read **U.S. POSTAL SERVICE** at one time, but judging by the old man standing in front of him, Einstein thought the one word that remained seemed just as appropriate. "What happened to your uniform?" he asked suspiciously.

"I'm wearing it, sonny," Greeley replied.

The old man's withered finger pointed at what remained of the Twinkie and Einstein panicked. Was Greeley expecting some sort of tip for rescuing him from his sleeping bag? All Einstein had to offer him was three dollars and a half-eaten Twinkie. Reluctantly, he offered Greeley the rest of his Twinkie. It seemed the least that he could do after the old guy had saved him from suffocating to death.

"No, thanks," Greeley said, shaking his head. "Junk food gives me gas."

Einstein sighed with relief as the postman walked over to the nightstand next to his cot and picked up the letters that he had written to his parents the day before. Like everything else at Creepy Time, mailboxes and stamps were in short supply. In fact, they didn't exist at all, keeping with the camp policy of no communication with the outside world. Obviously, Greeley was not aware of the policy or had decided to ignore it. Either way, Einstein figured he had nothing to lose and decided to play along.

"You want me to mail these for you, Houdini?"

"I don't have any stamps. Think you can help me out?" Einstein pleaded. "My life depends on these letters getting to the designated recipients."

Greeley swiped his bony thumb across the soot-covered window and pressed down on the top right-hand corner of the white envelope, leaving a ridged imprint. He took out a red felt pen and scrawled 39 *cents* beneath the greasy black thumbprint and then initialed it to make it official. He took the second letter and repeated the process.

"Is that legal?" Einstein asked.

"It is around these parts," Greeley answered. "If I use the full handprint, it goes out first class, guaranteed two-hour delivery. You in a hurry?"

"No, thanks," Einstein replied, realizing that the postman may be a few cards shy of a full deck.

The old man turned and slowly ambled toward the door, raising his wrinkled right hand toward the ceiling to signal his good-bye.

"Thanks for everything," Einstein shouted at Greeley's back.

"Don't mention it, sonny." He stopped at the door, then turned and smiled at Einstein. "Want to see a real magic trick, Houdini?"

"Sure," Einstein replied.

The man cackled again and walked straight through a solid oak door without opening it. Einstein ran to the front door and opened it, shocked to see Greeley strolling leisurely down the path. "How did you do that?" he asked, genuinely impressed with the illusion.

Greeley turned around and winked at Einstein. "Nothing to it, my boy," he said as he vanished before Einstein's eyes. "The trick is simple. You just have to be dead."

Einstein was paralyzed with fear. If bunking with werewolves and spiders weren't enough to cope with, he now had to deal with a postal ghost that thought he was the camp mailman. He crawled back into his sleeping bag, zipped himself in, and screamed at the top of his lungs.

CHAPTER 11

Day Three — 10:27 A.M.

Both the indoor and outdoor activities at Creepy Time were limited at best. The long list of boasts in the brochure simply didn't exist. Swimming and canoeing were completely out of the question, unless one had a death wish. There were no horses, which eliminated horseback riding. After the flaming marshmallow fight that broke out during orientation, Big Al had nixed all future events that involved gathering around a roaring campfire, including the traditional sing-alongs and weenie roasts. The arts and crafts center specialized in making lanyard key chains, basket weaving, and building birdhouses out of Popsicle sticks, activities that seemed more appropriate for a mental institution than a summer camp. Other than that, there wasn't much else to do at Creepy Time except for a torturous game that Bucky claimed to have invented. He called it Capture the Flag.

It was a simple game with simple rules. Two teams squared off in the middle of an open field and wrestled for control of the flag. The first team to impale the flag on a wooden post on the opposite side of the field won the game. The trick was to maneuver past the other players without getting tagged. Once players were tagged, they were out of the game for good.

Given the hellish temperature of the Mojave Desert in the middle of July, the game was not without danger. Despite salt tablets and sunblock, second-degree burns were as common as heat rash, and several of the players on each team would routinely collapse from dehydration at some point during the contest. The playing area was roughly the size of a football field. The terrain of sun-baked earth was hard and unforgiving. Cactus stumps and rocks littered the field like an obstacle course. The players with minor cuts and bruises were forced to endure the pain. Even those with more serious injuries were bandaged up on the sidelines and sent right back to the game.

Of the limited choice of activities that the camp had to offer, this one ranked at the bottom of the barrel, at least as far as Einstein was concerned. What was the logic of charging up and down a vacant lot to capture a four-by-twelve-inch rag while being chased by a band of screaming lunatics? Clearly, whoever invented this sadistic blood sport must have enjoyed the sight of human suffering. Einstein nibbled at a half-eaten Twinkie, fortifying himself for the ordeal that lay ahead.

"Yo, Fleet! Put down the cupcake and get your butt on that field!" Bucky shouted.

"I haven't had a decent meal in two days. Look at me!" he said, pulling the waistband of his pants about half an inch away from his belly. "I'm already showing signs of malnutrition. If you don't mind, I think I'll sit this one out."

"That right?" Bucky the human beaver said with a toothy

grin. "You don't look like you're starving to me. In fact, I'd say that you need that Twinkie 'bout as much as a bald man needs a blow-dry. If you ain't on that field in five seconds, Fleet, you'll be wearing that pastry for a hat!"

Einstein grudgingly returned what remained of the Twinkie back into the wrapper and slowly made his way toward the center of the playing field.

"And don't think I forgot about that costume either," Bucky shouted after him.

A shrill whistle blew and suddenly the game was afoot. Einstein watched the activity with detached fascination. The teams were divided into two distinct sides—werewolves versus mummies—which was only logical. Vinnie and the other vampires shunned the game altogether, preferring to stay in character and avoid direct sunlight. Werewolves and mummies ran about aimlessly, taunting one another with a relish that completely eluded Einstein. He eyed the players on the field and wondered which would be the first to collapse from heat prostration. The werewolves must have made a group decision to redo their outfits. They had cut off the sleeves of their plaid flannel shirts and chopped their pant legs off just below the knee. Einstein wasn't sure if he was imagining things or not, but the werewolves seemed to be even hairier than the night before. They looked like Neanderthal lumberjacks. The mummies had also decided to adapt their attire to the sweltering conditions of the desert. Ignoring the threat from Big Al, they had removed all of the bandages except for those covering their faces in favor of shorts and T-shirts that were more practical under the circumstances. As a result, the campers now looked like they had suffered head injuries.

"Wanna help me stick it to the werewolves, Fleet?" Roxie asked, tugging on his shirttail.

Einstein was disappointed to see that Roxie had adopted the official mummy team attire. If she hadn't spoken, Einstein wouldn't have recognized her at all. Before he could express his disapproval about her joining the status quo, she was already gone. He watched her jog down the field with purpose, shocked that a sophisticate such as she actually enjoyed this type of mindless dribble.

"Play on, comrade," Einstein shouted to Roxie. "I'll stay behind and bring up the rear."

Once the game had moved to the far end of the field, Einstein headed for the sideline. He found refuge beneath the rotting skeleton of an old wooden shed that had been abandoned and left in the desert to die. The structure appeared to be unstable, but it beat standing in the sun, toasting like a Pop-Tart in a microwave oven. Einstein pulled what remained of the half-eaten Twinkie out of his shirt pocket and picked up where he had left off before he was so rudely interrupted. The cream filling had melted and dribbled down his chin like a river, covering his shirt and hands with sticky white goop. As he wolfed down the last of the Twinkie, Einstein heard an odd humming sound coming from directly behind him. It seemed to be emanating from a small brown object that looked like a rotten pineapple, camouflaged and hanging precariously from a rotting wooden plank located in a dark crevice at the top corner of the shed. As Einstein got up, a loose board fell and the brown object burst to life. Suddenly, a horde of angry yellow jackets attacked from every direction.

Einstein jogged down the field as fast as his legs would carry him, with the insects in hot pursuit. Attracted by the sugary remains of the Twinkie, they stuck to Einstein like glue. He zigzagged down the field, trying to escape, but was unable to lose the angry insects. As Einstein charged toward the middle of the playing field, he ran smack dab into Billy the Werewolf. Billy was headed in the opposite direction, carrying the flag and making his way toward the end zone. They collided head-on, with Billy taking the brunt of the impact. Einstein grabbed the flag out of the dazed werewolf's hand and continued down the field, swatting at anything that was within swatting distance.

Counselors and campers alike watched the spectacle in awe.

"Now that's what I'm talking about," Bucky screamed, not noticing the source of Einstein's newfound motivation. "Look at him go! That boy got some skills!"

Einstein charged down the field like a bull, with the angry wasps in hot pursuit, mowing down anyone who got in his path. Both werewolves and mummies scurried out of his way to avoid being trampled to death. Only Roxie stood her ground and watched helplessly as the yellow jackets pursued Einstein down the field.

"Run for your life, Fleet!" Roxie shouted.

Einstein did just that until he reached the end zone and finally ran out of gas. There was no choice but to stand his ground and fight. He swatted at the swarm of insects with the flag, which only made matters worse. The more he swatted, the more agitated the wasps became. Einstein let out a bloodcurdling scream as he felt the razor-sharp teeth penetrate the seat of his shorts and sink deeply into his rear end. Instinctively, he grabbed the yellow jacket and tried to squish it, then quickly realized his mistake as the enraged insect repeatedly bit his palm. He jumped up and down and howled in pain, swatting the flag at anything that moved. Einstein fought the angry horde with every ounce of energy he had left. From the other end of the field it looked like a primitive victory dance of sorts, or early signs of dementia. Beaten and out of breath, Einstein knew that he had lost the battle—but it didn't mean that he had to lose the war.

"If you gotta go," Einstein gasped, "you might as well go out a winner." He held up the white flag for everyone to see, impaled it on the enemy goalpost, and then collapsed from exhaustion. As he lay curled up in a ball, his fellow teammates danced and cheered at their victory, chanting Einstein's name over and over again. Billy picked himself up from the ground and dusted himself off, snarling at his teammates.

"Way to go, Fleet," Bucky shouted from across the field. "Someone get that boy a salt tablet!"

CHAPTER 12

Day Three — 1:24 P.M.

Big Al's office was stark and well suited to the man's personality. A large metal desk sat in front of a few uncomfortable metal chairs. The empty bookshelf at the far end of his office was missing one leg and tilted like the Leaning Tower of Pisa. Big Al had selected the space because it was located at the end of the main building and was reasonably private. Not that it mattered anyway. After the incident at orientation, most of the campers were scared to death of Big Al and avoided him like the plague.

Big Al called the meeting to order by simply standing up and clearing his throat. The others immediately stopped what they were doing and waited for him to continue.

"I would like to begin by congratulating you all on a job well done," Big Al began, creating a positive atmosphere for the staff meeting. "Everything is running according to schedule and I'm pleased with the results."

He was a seasoned leader and knew the value of a good pat on the back.

"I picked up the mail at the P.O. box today," Bucky said, dropping an envelope on the table.

"That's it?" Big Al asked, shaking his head in amazement.

"That's it," Bucky confirmed. "Pretty pathetic, but it's more or less to be expected. These kids are all spoiled brats, misfits, and malcontents. Let's face it, that's why they're here. Their parents were happy to unload them for the summer and take off."

Big Al opened the envelope and removed a check for one hundred dollars made out to a kid named Manny. There was no note to accompany the check. The rule was no outside communication and Big Al was a stickler when it came to the rules. "Have any of the campers attempted to communicate with their parents?" he asked.

Bucky shook his head.

The situation was sad but true. The complete lack of communication required in the brochure was no doubt a selling point in the decision to send kids to Creepy Time.

"That's good," Big Al said. "It makes our job a lot easier."

"I don't know why we wasted the time and money to create that phony brochure," Curly said, giggling. "This group would have sent their kids to San Quentin for eight weeks and paid extra for solitary confinement."

Everyone laughed loudly except for the nurse.

"What is it?" Big Al asked.

"Curly messed up my name tag," she complained. "I think he did it on purpose. Everyone in camp thinks my name is Nurse Knockwurst."

"Knockwurst. Norkhurst. What's the difference?" Curly replied. "Neither one of them is your real name anyhow."

She gave Curly the evil eye. The cook threw his hands in the air and looked around the room for support.

"What is a knockwurst, anyway?" she asked.

"It's a big bloated weenie," Curly replied, smiling. "Hey, if the name tag fits."

"I'll wipe that smirk off your face, you pasty-faced little troll." She lunged across the table and grabbed Curly by the throat. Big Al and Bucky watched her strangle the cook until he turned blue. She pulled Curly up close and looked him in the eye. "I'm going to tie you to a tree and feed you to the scorpions."

"Good idea," Bucky said. "I second the motion."

"All in favor of tying Curly to a tree, say aye," Big Al said, enjoying the look of terror on the cook's face.

Everyone in the room held up their hands and shouted "Aye" at the top of their lungs.

"The ayes have it," Big Al announced, smiling at Curly. "Who has some rope?"

The room was silent and filled with anticipation as the sweat began to pour down the nervous cook's face. Curly dropped to his knees and begged for mercy. The room erupted in laughter once more, with Nurse Knockwurst laughing the loudest.

"We're just having a bit of fun with you, sport." Big Al leaned across the table and stared at the cook. "For now."

He lingered in Curly's face long enough to make certain that the cook got his message loud and clear, motioned for Nurse Knockwurst to release him, then pressed on with other business. "Is there anything else that I should know about?"

Curly wiped the sweat from his brow with a gravy-stained sleeve and sighed in relief.

"The Fleet kid may be a problem," Bucky reported. "I can't

find a werewolf costume that fits and he refuses to take his salt tablets."

"Won't take his salt tablets, eh?" Big Al replied, his eyes narrowing to small slits.

"He's a real pain in the butt," Curly said, confirming the fact. "I put some in his lunch yesterday and the little wimp accused me of trying to poison him. Claims that his uncle is the head of the Food and Drug Administration. One phone call from him and they'll shut down my kitchen."

"Where is the boy now?" Big Al asked.

"In the infirmary recovering from heatstroke," Bucky replied.

"Leave him to me," Nurse Knockwurst said.

Big Al smiled at her and nodded.

"I'm afraid that the Fleet kid isn't our only problem," Bucky reported.

"What is our other problem?" Big Al asked gruffly.

"We have a couple of runaways."

CHAPTER 13

Day Three — 1:55 P.M.

The Whammy sisters wandered aimlessly down the road, dragging their suitcases behind them. The dirt path was full of potholes and rocks. Both girls wished they had worn sneakers instead of designer boots with three-inch spiked heels. The black shoes looked very stylish with the witch outfits but were completely impractical under the circumstances. It gave a whole new meaning to the term *fashion victim*.

Willow signaled for her sister to stop and snatched the Official Trail Guide from her hands. She dusted off her Louis Vuitton suitcase and plopped herself down on top of it, intently studying the "simple" set of directions that showed the layout of the camp and the way to the main road. After three days of Creepy Time, the sisters had had enough of life in the wilderness. The last straw was when Curly had demanded that they turn in their witch outfits, put on the mummy costumes that they were supposed to wear in the first place, and get with the program. The sisters had other ideas. They decided to escape and spend the rest of the summer partying with their friends and trashing their parents' house instead. It wouldn't begin to even the score with their folks for sending them to this slum of a summer camp, but it was a good start.

"This map reads like an algebra assignment," Willow complained, turning the map upside down to see if she was missing something.

"You mean we're, like, totally lost?" Wanda asked.

"Duh . . . what do you think?" her twin replied, pointing at the endless sea of sand and sagebrush that surrounded the girls in all directions.

"We should have stayed with the rest of the witches," her twin replied.

"*Hola,* we're, like, the only witches in the whole stupid camp," Willow reminded her. "Can you believe that idiotic bus driver wanted us to wear those dirty rags? Yeah, like I'm going to cover my face in used gauze and hide my new nose job."

"Too bad we don't have our cell phones with us. Then we could have called for the bellboy and a taxi," Wanda insisted. "It's, like, so degrading to carry your own luggage."

"I hate to break this to you, sis," Willow said, not bothering to hide the sarcasm, "but this isn't exactly the Four Seasons."

"It was supposed to be," Wanda sobbed. "The pictures in the brochure were beautiful. This place is a total pit. We should sue."

Wanda sat down on a rock and pouted. It was one thing to get lost in the mall, but it was quite another to get lost in the desert. The worst that could happen in the mall was that they missed the chance to max out their father's credit cards. *This* was scary.

"I'm hungry and thirsty and I need to take a soak in a hot peppermint bubble bath," Willow whined. "This place sucks. I can't wait to get home."

"Me too," her sister agreed, wishing they had never set eyes on that stupid brochure. "This isn't a camp. It's a reform school. Sure, Mom and Dad pack up and spend the summer on the Riviera. We get eight weeks on the set of *Fear Factor*. It's totally unfair."

"This place stinks," Willow announced, holding her nose.

"For sure," Wanda agreed.

"No, I mean it, like, really stinks."

The odor was pungent, like the stink of rotting flesh. Willow covered her mouth with her hand, fighting back the urge to retch, and then she realized the source of the stench. She stared, unable to take her eyes off the gruesome scene.

"What is it?" Wanda inquired, noticing her sister had turned an ashen shade. "You look like you're going to hurl."

Willow pointed at the putrefied corpse that lay about ten feet to the left of the rock that her sister was perched upon. Maggots and scorpions were feeding on the carcass. Wanda jumped up and ran over to her sister. They held each other tightly and whimpered.

"Gro-oss," Wanda said, taking a one-syllable word and turning it into two.

"You think a coyote did this?" Willow asked.

"That *is* a coyote," Wanda answered softly.

"If that's a coyote . . . ," Willow muttered, letting the question linger.

"Then what killed the coyote?" Wanda replied, finishing the thought.

The answer was just over the ridge, hidden behind a rock. It moved swiftly and quietly, circling behind them, cutting off any chance to escape.

Wanda squeezed Willow tightly to her body. "If you scream in the desert," she asked her sister, "do you think anyone will hear you?"

No one did.

CHAPTER

Day Four — 4:34 P.M.

Einstein woke up feeling groggy and light-headed. His body ached and his skin itched like crazy. He made a clumsy attempt to scratch the back of his neck but found it difficult to do so. Both of his hands were bandaged. Slowly, he began to piece things together. Einstein remembered the wasps and shuddered. As the cobwebs in his head cleared, the room came into focus. It was stark and minimal and smelled like ammonia. White antiseptic walls, cots with white cotton sheets, and white tile floors. It could only be one place. Einstein was in the infirmary.

"Look who's back in the land of the living," a voice gently cooed. "We were very concerned about you, young man. You've been out cold for over a day."

Einstein turned to the sound of her voice and saw the camp nurse standing next to his bed, smiling like a mental patient. She was just as large and homely as Einstein remembered her to be, and the plain white uniform did little to improve her situation. Her greasy brown hair was wrapped into an over-sized bun, which rose out of the top of her nurse's cap like a skyscraper. "Nurse Knockwurst?"

"I told you my name is Norkhurst!" she growled with the bedside manner of Medusa.

The name tag was still pinned to her uniform, but Einstein was too weak to argue. "What happened to me?" he asked.

"You are suffering from dehydration in addition to experiencing an allergic reaction to the wasp bites. It's nothing serious. Take two of these and call me in the morning." Nurse Knockwurst snorted at her own joke as she tossed a couple of salt tablets at Einstein. Salt tablets seemed to be the prescribed cure for any and all types of sickness. Be it a headache, a bellyache, a wasp bite, a sprained ankle, food poisoning, malaria, or the common cold, the salt tab was the standard camp panacea for all that ailed you. Einstein flatly refused the offer, explaining that it was a well-known medical fact that salt clogged your arteries.

"You wouldn't happen to have a Twinkie?" Einstein inquired hopefully.

"You need to lay off the Twinkies, tubby," she replied, patting him playfully on the tummy. "Take the salt tablets."

"No, thanks," Einstein said, again rejecting the offer.

"You're being very naughty," the nurse scolded. "How do you expect to get better if you won't take your medicine?"

Einstein tuned her out as she continued to push the salt tab treatment, distracted by two of his fellow campers who were sitting up in their cots, quietly engrossed in a game of checkers. They were bandaged from head to toe. The only spots that Nurse Knockwurst had missed were small slits around their eyes and noses. "It's your move, Manny," one camper reminded the other.

"What happened to those guys?" Einstein whispered.

"Poison ivy."

"What did they do, roll in the stuff?"

"You can't be too careful," the nurse told Einstein.

Einstein took a closer look at Manny's frightened eyes and thought he recognized him as the poor soul on the bus that Billy Armstrong had pelted in the head with his Twinkie. The mummy costume that he'd arrived in the first day was nothing compared to the job that Nurse Knockwurst had done on him. His original costume was made of thin layers of soft white gauze that loosely covered his T-shirt and shorts. Thick layers of painter's tape had replaced the thin layers of gauze and were held tightly in place with several strands of electrician's tape. The black-and-blue color scheme looked like a giant bruise. "It seems a bit extreme if you ask me," Einstein said.

"Who asked, you insolent little twerp?" Nurse Knockwurst growled. For the next thirty minutes, she attempted to force-feed Einstein the salt tablets. Finally, having had enough of the cat-and-mouse game, Einstein bit her. The nurse stormed into her office in the back of the infirmary, screaming something about death and dismemberment before she slammed the door shut behind her. Einstein was not sorry to see her go. He retrieved pencil and paper from his pack and quickly jotted a note to describe the abysmal conditions in the infirmary.

"How they hangin', Houdini?" Greeley asked, materializing out of thin air.

Einstein pulled the covers over his head and hoped the ghost would disappear. He considered the possibility that Greeley was only a figment of his imagination and that he may be suffering from sunstroke or a brain tumor. It was not the first time that he'd been accused of being crazy, but it was the first time that he considered the possibility. He waited a few moments and then took a peek to see if the coast was clear. Greeley was still standing next to the bed, grinning at him. "Go haunt someone else, Greeley!" Einstein snapped.

"Sounds like someone woke up on the wrong side of the cot," Greeley replied, suppressing a soft chuckle. He eyed the welt marks that covered Einstein's face and arms with genuine concern. "What happened to you?"

"I attempted to escape," Einstein replied. As much as he hated to admit it, he was actually happy to see someone other than Nurse Knockwurst and the mummies, even if it was a ghost or just a figment of his own imagination. "Camp management roughed me up a bit as an object lesson to the others. I'm thinking about filing a lawsuit."

"You don't say," Greeley said with more than a hint of sarcasm in his voice. "Looks like the work of some real pros. What did they use on you? Lit cigarette butts?"

"Trained killer bees," Einstein replied, yawning to show his indifference to the matter.

"Killer bees, huh? Well, I bet that hurt like the dickens."

"I've been trained to endure pain," Einstein told the postman. "Last summer my parents sent me to boot camp in Bosnia."

Greeley ignored the comment and pointed at the bandaged campers. "That lady sure does enjoy her work. Back in my day, we didn't have a camp nurse or an infirmary. If you got hurt, you were lucky to get a Band-Aid."

"You went to camp?" Einstein said, somewhat surprised. He tried to picture Greeley roasting marshmallows and singing songs around a campfire, but it wasn't easy.

"I guess you could say that," the ghost replied. "I used to own this place. Built it from the ground up in 1962."

"*You* owned Camp Creepy Time?" Einstein asked skeptically, wondering if Greeley was telling the truth or just having a senior moment.

"It was called Camp Sleepy Time back then," Greeley said softly. "There was a stable full of horses and riding paths. We taught all the kids to ride and put on a rodeo at the end of every summer. The lake was stocked with all sorts of fish and the swimming pool was always clean. We had a crafts center with artists who taught the kids how to paint and build birdhouses. The kitchen was clean and the grub was top-drawer. You should have seen this place back in the day. Sleepy Time was a great place to spend the summer, and then it happened."

"What happened?" Einstein asked.

"I don't want to talk about it," Greeley replied, his eyes filled with anger. "I lost the camp along with everything else that I owned and became a postman."

"From the sultan of Sleepy Time to a slave of the United States Postal Service," Einstein said, feeling sorry for the old man. "Can I ask you a personal question?"

The ghost nodded.

"Why are you still here?"

"To tell you the truth, I don't know," Greeley replied, scratching his head. "One minute I was standing around minding my own beeswax and the next minute I was dead, run over by my own pickup truck."

"Sentenced to death without parole," Einstein said, thinking out loud. "That's a tough break."

Greeley patted Einstein softly on the head. "You're all right, Houdini."

Einstein handed the ghost an envelope that contained his latest letter. "Can you mail this for me?" he whispered.

"Regular or priority mail?" the dead postman asked. It was clear that Greeley took his job quite seriously, although Einstein had his doubts about whether the letter would ever reach its destination.

"Regular would be just fine, thanks."

Greeley licked his thumb and rubbed it across the seat of his trousers. He held the bony digit a few inches from his face, inspecting it carefully to make sure it was covered with a sufficient amount of dirt to create a smudge mark on the corner of the envelope.

"You're all set," Greeley announced as he ground his thumbprint into the paper.

"Do you mind if I ask you another personal question?" Einstein asked, without waiting for Greeley to answer. "How can you deliver a letter without using a stamp?"

"Nothing to it," Greeley replied. "I use g-mail."

"You have an account with Google?"

The old postman looked confused. "I use ghost mail. It's the same principle as e-mail, but it's guaranteed to be spam free and you don't have to pay a dime. Being dead has its perks."

Einstein thought nanotechnology was the next great inno-vation, but a technology based on the metaphysical? He had a thousand questions for the old man. "How does g-mail work?"

"Just like that gizmo they used on *Star Trek*," Greeley replied. "I can move anything I touch from one location and transport it instantaneously to another."

"Would you do me a favor?" Einstein whispered.

"Sure, Houdini. What do you need?"

"Beam me up, Scotty! I want to go home."

"You're not going anywhere in your condition," Nurse Knockwurst said, cutting in on the conversation. She placed her hand on the boy's forehead to see if he was running a fever. "You're delirious."

"I feel fine."

"Really?" Nurse Knockwurst asked. "Then why have you been jabbering to yourself for the last five minutes?"

"I'm talking to Greeley, the camp mailman," Einstein said indignantly. "And if you don't mind, we were having a pri-vate conversation."

"Isn't that cute," the nurse said loud enough for everyone in the room to hear. "Einstein has an imaginary friend."

"He's not imaginary. He's a ghost."

"What's the difference?" Nurse Knockwurst said as she jammed a thermometer into Einstein's mouth. She strolled back into her office, returned with a standard-issue werewolf costume, and tossed it to Einstein. "Bucky brought this by while you were sleeping. Try it on and see how it fits."

"I'm not feeling up to playing dress-up just yet," Einstein said, brushing the wolf suit aside.

She yanked the thermometer out of his mouth and checked the reading. "Your temperature is normal. Unfortunately, you are not." Nurse Knockwurst threw another handful of salt tablets on the bed and glared at Einstein. "I'm tired of playing games. I'm going out for twenty minutes and if you're not wearing that wolf getup by the time I get back, you and your imaginary friend are both going to regret it."

"Don't listen to her, Houdini," Greeley warned.

"I wasn't planning on it, but thanks anyhow for the advice," Einstein replied as he watched Nurse Knockwurst head for the door.

The nurse stopped in her tracks and, without bothering to turn around, screamed at the top of her lungs, "Will you please stop talking to yourself? It's driving me crazy!"

Nurse Knockwurst mumbled something under her breath and then stormed out of the room.

"There is something wrong with that woman," Einstein whispered.

"You have no idea," the ghost replied.

CHAPTER
15

Day Four — 8:13 P.M.

Curly's bad cooking was one thing, but the aftereffects were something else altogether. Diarrhea (or "Curly's Revenge," as it was commonly referred to by everyone trapped at Creepy Time) had spread through the camp population like wildfire. The bathrooms at the dining hall were insufficient to deal with the crowds that inevitably gathered after each and every meal. Some days it was so bad that the lines were stacked up all the way back to the fire pit outside the cafeteria.

One camper who was in dire straits ran back to his cabin to find a toilet that was not currently in use, but he was disappointed. Not only was the bathroom occupied, but there was also a line of fidgeting campers waiting for a chance to use one of the two stalls. Unable to hold it, he decided on desperate measures.

"Throw me some TP," he screamed at the guy in the front of the line.

"You're not thinking about going out there," the other camper replied, pointing toward the moonlit desert. "What about Godzilla?"

Every summer camp develops its own particular brand of

campfire lore that is intentionally invented to scare the wits out of the campers, and Camp Creepy Time was no exception. During the first few days there, many of the kids claimed that they had seen a pony-sized spider covered in matted red fur. The descriptions of the creature varied, but a few of the facts remained constant. It had several bulbous eyes that were perched on the tip of tentacles that sprouted from the top of its head. Rows of large yellow fangs jutted out its mouth like a great white shark's, and its jaws were so powerful that they were capable of shredding steel. The stories spread and began to take on a life of their own. Einstein theorized that the creature was some type of indigenous spider mutated by toxic waste. Naturally, the toxic waste had been dumped in the desert by either the government or by a large conglomerate with no respect for Mother Nature. There were several names for the creature, but only one stuck. Godzilla.

"I don't care if King Kong is out there," the boy screamed. "Just toss me some TP and I'll take my chances."

The boy caught the roll on the fly and headed for the privacy of the desert. He squatted behind a large tumbleweed and sighed loudly with relief. The rustling sound a few feet away told him that he wasn't the only desperate soul.

"Food really sucks here, doesn't it?" he said, trying to make light of an embarrassing situation.

There was no answer, but someone was definitely there.

"Beats my mom's home cooking," the boy added, hoping a bit of humor would break the ice. "If you consider Chinese takeout home cooking."

The joke didn't elicit a response and the silence was starting to make the boy nervous. He supposed that one of the other campers was playing a practical joke on him, but this wasn't funny. No one likes to get caught with his pants down, especially at a time like this.

"Take a hike!" the boy shouted angrily.

He stood and pulled his pants up, deciding that waiting in line was a better option than being spied on by some camp pervert. As the boy started back for the cabin, he heard the sound of something large shuffling through the underbrush. It was heading straight for him. He started to run as fast as his legs would carry him, but it wasn't fast enough. The camper felt something wrap around his feet and he tripped. He screamed at the top of his lungs as he was dragged into the brush. Then there was silence.

"Did you hear that?" one of the campers said to another camper waiting to use the latrine. "Poor guy sounds like he's dying."

The camper nodded in agreement and grimaced.

"Hey, when you gotta go, you gotta go."

CHAPTER 16

Day Five — 6:25 P.M.

Norman Fleet was in the middle of watching the nightly news when he heard the doorbell ring. He went to the front door to see who it was, but there was no one. Once again, a white envelope addressed to "The Fleet Family" was sitting on the welcome mat. It was another letter from Einstein. Aside from the content itself and the fact that no one ever saw the delivery person, there was something very strange about the whole thing. The letters showed up on the doorstep without a stamp or any other visible means of payment. Norman Fleet supposed that a five-star camp like Creepy Time must have contracted with an upscale private delivery service and let it go at that. Nonetheless, it was a bit odd.

He took his son's letter to his favorite easy chair. Norman adjusted the footrest and leaned back as he opened the goo-stained envelope, eager to hear about camp. A smile came to his face as he recalled his own childhood memories of roasting weenies and marshmallows over an open campfire and singing songs under a sky full of stars. The smile quickly vanished as he read the first few lines of the letter.

Dear Mom and Dad,

Help!!!!!!!!

Camp management continues to torture us on a daily basis. Just yesterday, we were forced (at gunpoint) to run half naked through a field while the staff placed bets on which one of us would drop first. After being ordered to strip down to our underwear, our bodies were coated in honey. Little did we know that the counselors had trained enormous wasps to attack on their command. My earlier dispute with camp management naturally made me a prime target. As a result, I was stung over 600 times (a new camp record) and have spent the last two days in a coma.

The warden and his lackeys have imprisoned me in the camp infirmary and placed me under around-the-clock surveillance (excluding bathroom breaks). Nurse Knockwurst (aka Dr. Frankenstein) is as sadistic a fiend as this camp has to offer. Aside from being mentally unstable, I suspect that Nurse Knockwurst is wanted in several states for practicing medicine without a license. Everyone who ends up in her infirmary is treated like a lab rat. Two campers have been subjected to some type of bizarre medical experiment and are slowly turning into mindless zombies. In all fairness to the camp nurse, they may have been like this before arriving at Creepy

Time, but at least they weren't bound to their cots.

Nurse Knockwurst's insistence on the liberal use of salt tablets for any ailment is in line with camp policy. In response to her daily efforts to force-feed medicine against my will, I have gone on a hunger strike. I will not eat again until Nurse Knockwurst's reign of terror is put to an end or camp management adds Twinkies to the menu.

On top of everything else they forgot to mention in the brochure, it appears that we have a resident ghost at Creepy Time. His name is Greeley. The cantankerous old coot claims to be both mailman and master of the manor. I suspect that he is just some dead guy with delusions of grandeur. Of course, since I'm the only one who can see Greeley, it may be my own problem.

There is something rotten at Creepy Time, aside from just the food. A few desperate souls decided to make a break for it and have been missing ever since. The word is that someone or something ate the missing campers, but I suspect that camp management planted the story to deter future attempts at escape. If I survive my stay in the infirmary, I plan to get to the bottom of it. In the meantime, please send some more Twinkies. It's hard to think on an empty stomach.

Sincerely,
Einstein P. Fleet

Shirley Fleet walked into the living room just as her husband finished reading the letter. She was carrying a large platter of freshly baked chocolate chip cookies.

"Is that another letter from Einstein?" Shirley asked, sampling one of the cookies.

Norman leaned back in his easy chair and nodded. "It's more like a handwritten blog."

"Is he having a good time yet?" she asked.

Norman handed her the letter. She read the first few lines and began to giggle.

"Trained killer bees and campfire conspiracies," she said, laughing out loud. Shirley put down the letter and picked up another cookie. "You gotta admit that our little guy has some imagination."

"His imagination almost got us arrested," Norman replied. "Or have you forgotten about the Wilson incident already?"

Mr. Wilson was Einstein's fourth-grade history teacher. For reasons that no one but Einstein could understand, he was convinced that the man was part of a "sleeper cell" that had been sent by the forces of darkness to study the decaying school system in Los Angeles and replicate it throughout the country. The plot was to make America stupid. Einstein posted daily blogs on *The Smoking Peashooter* to warn anyone who would listen. An overzealous FBI agent in the counterterrorism division acted on the information and arrested the poor man. As it turned out, all Mr. Wilson was guilty of was changing his last name from Wilnofski to Wilson, but his motives were hardly sinister. His new name was easier for the kids to pronounce. The FBI released Wilson a few days later, but his lawsuit against the federal government and the Fleets was still pending.

Shirley walked across the room and handed her husband the plate. "Relax, Norman. Have a cookie."

"Only Einstein could turn summer camp into a corporate conspiracy. If he keeps this up, they will probably give him the boot—which is exactly what he wants."

"Give him a call and have a talk with him," his wife suggested.

"It's against camp rules. Besides, if Einstein thinks that we're buying into this nonsense, he's got another thing coming."

"So, what *do* we do?"

Norman considered the matter as he helped himself to a cookie. Suddenly he had an idea. Why not turn a bad situation into a golden brown opportunity? As the regional marketing director for Hostess, he could provide Einstein and the rest of the campers with an eight-week supply of Twinkies and write off the cost of camp as a marketing expense. They didn't call him "El Cheapo" for nothing.

"I'll call the office and have them send a couple dozen boxes of Twinkies," he said, winking at his wife. "Two can play at this game."

CHAPTER 17

Day Six — 5:30 A.M.

Vinnie looked at his watch and yawned. He'd been up all night. No wonder he was exhausted.

Over the past few days Vinnie had become extremely sensitive to sunlight. Every camper in V-Block seemed to be suffering from the same condition. As a result, they roamed the camp during the darkness of night and returned before sunrise. Oddly enough, the camp counselors did not seem to mind these nocturnal activities. Curly even set up a special midnight feeding at the camp cafeteria to accommodate their schedule. The menu of blood-rare meat was limited, but no one seemed to mind. Given their snow-white complexions from the lack of exposure to the sun, a little red meat couldn't hurt.

Vinnie had a terrible taste in his mouth and his breath smelled like rancid milk. He rifled his suitcase for his toothbrush and some toothpaste, then made his way to the sink at the end of the hall. Every single window was covered with blankets and anything else that would block out the sunlight. The cabin was pitch-black, but Vinnie had no problem navigating. His night vision improved with each passing day. He assumed it was from living like a mole in the darkness.

Vinnie turned on the faucet and squeezed a thick wad of toothpaste directly into his mouth. No matter how hard he brushed, the foul taste would not go away. After several minutes, he finally gave up and took a long swig of mouthwash. He held up his toothbrush and examined the bristles. They looked as if they'd been passed through a shredder. He inserted his index finger into his mouth and cut it on something sharp. His fake plastic fangs had been replaced with the real thing. He decided to call his father to let him know that he had contracted some rare strain of hoof-and-fang disease. Vinnie reached for his cell phone and remembered that he didn't have one at his disposal. Unable to procure dental advice, he took matters into his own hands. Leaning into the mirror, he examined his new canines. Vinnie could feel the sharpened fangs, but he couldn't see them. In fact, he couldn't see a thing. He was standing directly in front of the mirror, but no longer had a reflection.

"Vat in the name of good dental hygiene is going on here?" he mumbled, feeling the surface of the mirror, certain that it was some type of practical joke.

All of a sudden, Vinnie was overwhelmed by the need to go back to bed. Whatever the problem was, it would hold until later. Vinnie went to his cot and shut his eyes, but sleep was impossible. A symphony of clogged sinuses and snoring echoed throughout the cabin. He placed his pillow on top of his head to muffle the noise. After a few minutes he sat up and screamed at the top of his lungs, "Vill you keep it down over there? I'm trying to get some sleep!"

The symphony continued.

Vinnie got up and walked through the cabin. Something

87

wasn't right. He could hear his roommates snoring like chain saws, but they weren't in their cots. Vinnie looked up at the ceiling and gasped. The entire population of V-Block was sound asleep, hanging upside down from the rafters.

Vinnie felt an odd sensation course through his body. He began to float slowly toward the ceiling like a balloon filled with helium. He drifted until he came to an unoccupied spot and parked himself next to another camper, hanging upside down from the wooden rafter like the others. The odd sensation soon passed and Vinnie began to feel better. In fact, he had never felt better in his entire life. He felt strong and vibrant. His night vision was perfect, his hearing more acute, and his sense of smell had dramatically improved. The foul taste was worse than ever and his breath still smelled like rotten eggs, but it no longer bothered him in the least.

"I am Vinnie the Vampire!" he shouted. "I am immortal!"

"You vant to keep it down there, pal?" the vampire hanging next to him snarled. "You're not the only guy trying to get some sleep around here."

CHAPTER

18

Day Six — 4:55 P.M.

R ise and shine, comrade," Roxie demanded as she stood over the cot. Einstein had the blankets pulled tightly over his head and refused to move a muscle. She noticed that his clothes were strewn on the floor and he was moaning in his sleep. Perhaps Einstein was in worse shape than she thought. Roxie pulled back the blankets and gasped. Einstein was bound to the cot with electrician's tape. A werewolf mask was taped to his head, and his own clothes had been replaced with a plaid shirt and a pair of gray slacks. Roxie gently removed the tape and then struggled with the rubber mask until she finally pried it off. She pulled a dirty sock out of Einstein's mouth and used it to wipe the sweat from his brow.

"I really hate this place," Einstein said, rubbing the corners of his mouth. He sat up and stretched, but did not get out of bed.

"What happened?" Roxie asked as she opened her pocket-knife. She began to saw through the tape that bound his arms and legs, doing her best not to cut Einstein in the process.

"What do you think happened?" he answered testily. "Nurse Knockwurst, Bucky, Billy, and a few of the other Hitler Youth jumped me last night. They force-fed me a couple of salt tablets and gagged me so I couldn't spit them out. Then they stripped me down to my underwear and dressed me up as a werewolf. It was another fun-filled night at good old Camp Creepy Time. So, what did you do last night?"

"Did you swallow the salt tablets?" Roxie asked, clearly concerned.

"I didn't have much choice," Einstein replied. "I thought I was going to puke in my sleep and die, but I wasn't that fortunate."

"Remove that costume immediately," Roxie commanded. "Move it, Fleet. We have to get out of here and find a place to hide."

"Einstein P. Fleet does not hide," he replied indignantly.

"Is that right?" Roxie said. "Then what are you doing here?"

"I'm recovering."

"You look just fine to me," Roxie replied as she stripped the bed with him in it and tossed the blanket aside. Einstein hit the floor with a loud thud.

"Are you crazy?" Einstein shouted.

"Here you go, Fleet," Roxie said, tossing him his fishing cap and the rest of his clothes.

Einstein pulled the mosquito netting down over his face and stood there.

"Now what?" she asked.

"A little privacy, if you don't mind," he grumbled. "Unless you're looking for a cheap thrill."

Roxie scanned the infirmary as Einstein dressed. Nine other

cots were filled with injured campers, every one of them bandaged from head to toe. The parts that were still visible looked withered and gray, more like the skin of elephants than of human beings. The sick campers stared at Roxie. Their eyes were dead and lifeless.

"Let's go, Fleet."

"What's the hurry?" Einstein asked, tilting his cap to the side. "Are they running short of seats at the arts and crafts center?"

Einstein had been weighing his options for the past few minutes and was still undecided. Despite the hazing that he had suffered, staying in the infirmary had its advantages. If Einstein remained in the sick bay, he would be free of C-Block and his mentally defective roommates. He would have ample time to work on his planned exposé of Creepy Time for his website. Einstein was certain that his fellow bloggers would be appalled at the torture and use of experimental drugs on innocent campers in a laboratory disguised as a summer camp. Most important of all, Einstein would be freed from the physical rigors of day-to-day camp activities, such as they were. No more running aimlessly through an empty field while being baked to a crisp and chased by man-eating wasps. Granted, the food in the infirmary was the same hog slop they served in the camp cafeteria, but at least the bathroom line was shorter.

On the other hand, there was Nurse Knockwurst and a room full of sick campers bandaged like mummies to consider. The room was beginning to smell like rotting flesh and the constant moaning was driving him crazy. Worst of all, he was starving. Einstein hadn't eaten in days and recovering his stash of Twinkies required leaving the infirmary. He had to admit, it was not an easy decision.

"Hey, Manny," Einstein shouted across the room.

"Mmmmm?" the camper replied in a low, guttural moan that sounded more animal-like than human.

"You wouldn't happen to have something to eat over there, would you?"

"Mmmmm," Manny replied, slowly moving his head from side to side.

"This is an outrage!" Einstein shouted. "We have been incarcerated against our will and starved. We must organize, comrades. I'll draft a letter of protest to camp management and let them know that this is not acceptable. Even captured prisoners of war have rights under the Geneva Convention."

"Mmmmm," the mummies moaned in unison, nodding in agreement.

"Poor devils," Einstein whispered to Roxie. "They seem to have lost the power of speech. Did you notice that Nurse Knockwurst taped their hands and feet to the bedposts? She claims it keeps them from scratching their rashes raw. Now they can't even raise their hands to go to the bathroom, let alone ask permission. The woman is a complete quack and a disgrace to the medical profession. It's all in my report."

"We really don't have time for this, Fleet," Roxie persisted.

"What are you talking about?" he asked.

"I'll tell you later," she whispered. "The walls have ears."

Einstein looked around the room. Thanks to the handiwork of Nurse Knockwurst, there wasn't an ear in sight.

"How 'bout a Twinkie?" Roxie asked, watching his eyes light

up at the very mention of the word. "Golden brown, baked to perfection, oozing with cream in the center."

Einstein thought of the treasure trove of tasty treats that were wasting away in the walls of C-Block. His stomach began to gurgle and churn. After three long Twinkie-less days and nights, Einstein realized that the decision was really a no-brainer. He swung his hat around backward, removing the netting from his eyes.

"Let's go," he said, walking toward the door. "No fight was ever won on an empty stomach."

"That's the spirit," Roxie said. "I'm right behind you, comrade."

CHAPTER 19

Day Six — 5:22 P.M.

Curly the Cook placed the steaming hot bowl of earthworms, chopped wasp wings, and mashed butterfly gravy on the table and stepped back to admire his work. He added a bottle of Tabasco for flavor and sampled the dish again. It was perfect. "Come and get it while it's still moving," he shouted. "Dinner is served."

"You've outdone yourself, Curly," Big Al bellowed, savoring the aroma. Big Al tasted the thick gray sludge and smacked his lips. Years of training and discipline had taught him to improvise and adapt to any environment. Big Al had no clue what he was eating, nor did he care. The food was nutritious and could be foraged without leaving the camp.

"Thanks, boss."

Nurse Knockwurst and Bucky walked into the kitchen together. They both eyed the large bowl on the table, but remained standing. Bucky would have preferred a good steak or some fried chicken, but he knew the drill. He had been serving under Big Al for over ten years and he knew better than to question orders.

"Have some of this grub," Big Al said between swallows. "It's good."

Bucky tossed a wolf mask on the table. "We have a problem, boss. The Fleet kid escaped. We went by the infirmary to check on the mummies and he was gone."

"Imbeciles!" Big Al roared. "Did he take the mummies with him?"

"That's the weird part," Bucky replied quickly. He cast a nervous glance at Nurse Knockwurst before he continued. "They're right where we left them, taped to their cots."

"What are you getting at?" Big Al asked.

"If the mummies didn't help that boy escape, who did?" Bucky replied. "Somebody had to help him. I taped him to his cot just like the others."

"Maybe he's stronger than he looks," Curly suggested.

"The tape wasn't torn," Bucky said, shaking his head. "It was cut."

Big Al considered the situation from all angles. It was possible that the werewolves had attacked the infirmary, but unlikely. If they had, the tape would have been torn to shreds, along with the Fleet kid. Vinnie and Einstein seemed to get on well enough, but the incident had occurred in broad daylight, which eliminated the vampire as a suspect. Nevertheless, someone had to have helped the boy to escape. Eleven campers were missing and unaccounted for. In this type of operation a few casualties were to be expected, but eleven was more than the norm. Perhaps one of them was responsible for the escape. But why would they take the Fleet kid and leave everyone else behind? That was the million-dollar question.

"Did the boy have any visitors?" Big Al asked the nurse.

"One," Nurse Knockwurst replied. "He was very chummy with the camp mailman."

Everyone but the cook laughed.

"We don't have a camp mailman," Curly said, scratching his head. "Do we?"

"That's the point, you twit!" Nurse Knockwurst shouted. "The little brat made it all up. He invented this imaginary friend named Greeley to annoy me. The boy is disturbed."

"Did you say Greeley?" Big Al asked, his tone strange.

The nurse nodded.

"Name mean something to you?" Bucky asked.

"As you all know, Earth has been visited by extraterrestrials for thousands of years," Big Al said, avoiding the question. "For the most part, the visits went unnoticed. This all changed after two UFOs crashed in a town called Roswell. Both crews followed standard operating procedure and jettisoned their escape pods, leaving drones behind to fly the ship. The drones were found at the crash site."

"Which type?" Curly asked. "Pale and skinny with big eyes or short and green with big heads?"

"It's not important," Big Al grumbled. "What is important is the cover-up that followed. The government claimed that the crash and the discovery of alien life would set off a wave of panic, which was absurd. The real reason for the cover-up was that the government, along with several large corporations, was interested in the advanced technology, so they made a deal. They agreed to cover up all future alien activities on the planet in exchange."

"In exchange for what?" Curly asked. "Plasma televisions and cell phones?"

"The right to visit the planet and abduct a few of its citizens," Big Al replied, staring at the cook. "Naturally, there were conditions. A quota was placed on the number of abductions and all visits were limited to isolated, pre-approved locations."

"Places like Camp Creepy Time," Bucky said.

"That is correct," Big Al confirmed.

"I'm confused," Curly said. "What does any of this have to do with the Fleet kid's imaginary little friend?"

"Greeley might not be imaginary," Big Al replied. "He could be a ghost."

"What makes you think that?" Bucky asked.

"Because I'm the one who killed him."

CHAPTER

Day Six — 8:28 P.M.

Einstein and Roxie hiked to C-Block to liberate his stash of Twinkies. She had spent the last two hours trying to talk him out of it, but to no avail. Einstein was starving and irrational. As they approached the cabin, they heard an eerie howling sound in the distance. The closer they got to the cabin, the louder the howling became.

"Sounds like a pack of wild animals," Roxie whispered.

"That would be my bunkmates," Einstein replied, shaking his head in disgust.

Einstein stepped onto the patio and peeked through the window to make sure that the coast was clear. What he saw shocked him. Inside the cabin, there were seven werewolves sitting in a semicircle, eating *his* Twinkies and howling with delight.

"HEY! Those are my Twinkies!" Einstein growled as Roxie pulled him away from the window and out of sight.

"Are you nuts?" Roxie asked.

Einstein sighed with a hint of desperation. "I've been haunted, hazed, and haven't eaten in three days. And now this." He pointed at a werewolf with a cream-covered nose and shook his head. "It's Twinkie torture."

"You're losing it, Fleet."

As they watched through the window, the tallest of the werewolves stood up and took his place at the center of the semicircle. "Hey, Wally," he shouted across the room, "toss me another Twinkie."

Wally didn't seem to hear the request. Like the others, he was completely caught up in a heated debate. The werewolves seemed to be divided as to who would win in a *mano a mano* battle of the camp monsters. Apparently the Wolfman never did battle with the Mummy or Dracula in any of the old movies, so there was no real point of reference as to the outcome. The closest he had come was a cameo appearance in a 1971 flick called *Dracula vs. Frankenstein*.

"You guys make me sick," the tall werewolf snarled. "Are you werewolves or a bunch of little wussies?"

Wally looked up and shook his head. "I used to be like you," he said, sighing. "Angry all the time. Mad at the world. But after seven years of counseling I've learned to deal with those issues. You need to take a deep breath and embrace your inner werewolf."

"Embrace this," the tall werewolf growled. He picked Wally up and hurled him headfirst through the window. "Now, will someone toss me another Twinkie?"

"Is that Billy Armstrong?" Einstein whispered, visibly shocked by the change in the boy's appearance. His entire body was covered with thick brown fur. Muscular arms bulged out of the sawed-off sleeves of his plaid shirt. His calf muscles were just as thick. He looked like a hairy bodybuilder. Large fangs protruded from his mouth, yellow as ever and in need of a good brushing. The wind gusted and the smell of Billy's feet filled the air. It was definitely Billy. "Maybe he's been taking steroids or something. We'll report him to camp management and request immediate counseling."

Roxie stared at Einstein in disbelief. "You're kidding me, right?"

"Do you have a better explanation?" Einstein demanded.

"Just an obvious one," Roxie replied. "The campers are turning into monsters."

Einstein laughed. "Don't be ridiculous. It's a monster theme camp. The kids are wearing costumes. Think of them as character campers."

A flock of bats swarmed overhead. Einstein looked up and gasped as one of them waved its wing at him. It had a familiar human face and a bat body. It was Vinnie. "Vat's up, Einstein?" the vampire shouted as he flew by.

"Does that look like a costume to you?" Roxie asked.

Einstein was speechless. He looked back at the cabin and saw his old bunkmates for what they were. Werewolves. It suddenly dawned on Einstein that he was in a world of trouble. He didn't have the slightest clue why this was happening, but now wasn't the time to think about it. The only thing that mattered now was an exit strategy. "We have to escape immediately," he whispered.

"Get a grip, Fleet," Roxie replied. "It's ten miles to the nearest road and another twenty to the nearest town, all of it through a desert full of nocturnal predators. You wouldn't last an hour out there. I say we hide out for the night. If you still want to make a run for it, let's do it first thing in the morning. At least we'll stand a fighting chance."

"Where do you suggest we go?" Einstein asked.

"To the old caretaker's cottage out by the barn. We need to talk to a mutual friend."

"What mutual friend?" Einstein questioned.

"Greeley."

Her answer took him by surprise. No one could see the ghost other than Einstein. He was beginning to believe that Greeley was just a figment of his imagination. Obviously he was wrong on both counts. Before he could ask her to elaborate further, the howling of werewolves echoed through the desert night. The meeting was adjourned. They had polished off what was left of Einstein's Twinkies and were ready for the hunt. His questions would have to wait.

"Let's go, Fleet!"

Einstein and Roxie quietly retreated, quickly putting as much distance between themselves and the werewolves as possible. Once they were a safe distance from the cabin, Einstein stopped to catch his breath. He put his hands on his knees and sighed. "I can't believe the werewolves ate my Twinkies."

CHAPTER

21

Day Six — 9:01 P.M.

The caretaker's cottage was a stone's throw away from the old barn, just where Roxie said it would be. Some would describe it as rustic and cozy. Einstein thought it was cramped and claustrophobic, especially in the darkness. A large picture window faced the desert, but it was caked with a thick layer of dust and grime, making it impossible to enjoy the scenic view. Two easy chairs were positioned to face out the window, which seemed absurd under the circumstances. A smaller picture window had a direct view of the barn. A full moon lit up the desert but did very little to help the visibility inside the cabin. Instead it illuminated the room with a ghostly aura, which was only appropriate since the cottage was Greeley's home.

Einstein paced back and forth across the room, lost in his own thoughts. Roxie could see Greeley as clear as day and obviously knew the ghost, but had never bothered to mention it to Einstein. The question was why. Nurse Knockwurst didn't see the old man even though he was standing right in front of her. Or was it just an act? It was obvious that Roxie and Greeley were working together. But were they in bed with camp management? Someone had turned the campers into monsters and Einstein didn't know whom to trust. If he was going to survive, he had to stay alert.

"Be prepared, old boy," Einstein mumbled to himself. "Be prepared."

"What was that, Fleet?" Roxie asked.

"Nothing," he replied.

"Sit down and take a load off," the ghost said, pointing at one of the chairs. "*Mi casa es su casa.*"

Roxie walked over to the smaller window and rubbed a small section clean with a rag, scanning the area for any sign of activity. She handed Einstein her rhinestone-embedded cat glasses and told him to put them on. "Take a look."

He put on her glasses and looked outside. Everything was washed in a soft blue tint, but he was able to see perfectly. They were night goggles.

"If you want to zoom in on anything, push the red rhinestone at the top left corner," Roxie instructed. "The pink one beneath will adjust the focus."

"Where did you get these?" Einstein asked.

"Standard issue field glasses, courtesy of IMPS," Roxie replied.

"IMPS?"

"Intergalactic Monster Police Squad," Roxie replied. She pulled out a cheesy-looking badge and showed it to Einstein. He wasn't sure what to make of it. The tin-plated shield looked like a prize they'd give away in a box of Cracker Jack. "I've been after Big Al and his gang for the last three years. This is the closest that I've ever come to catching them."

"You work for the government?" Einstein gasped.

"You could say that," Roxie replied.

"Well, that explains everything." He had long suspected the existence of covert government agencies that operated under the radar—shadow organizations funded by two-hundred-dollar staplers and five-hundred-dollar toilet seats, all at the expense of unsuspecting taxpayers.

"What are you talking about, Fleet?"

"I'm talking about the unlawful use of experimental drugs to transform kids into monsters! I'm talking about a secret laboratory hidden in the middle of the Mojave Desert that was supposedly a summer camp! I'm talking about a subversive government plot funded by corrupt corporations to exploit innocent youth for the almighty buck! I'm talking about a major conspiracy right here at good old Camp Creepy Time!" Einstein shouted. "That's what *I'm* talking about!"

"Are you following any of this?" Greeley whispered to Roxie.

"Yeah," Roxie whispered back. "He thinks we're the bad guys."

The ghost turned to Einstein and looked him in the eye. "This isn't your fight, son. You want to go home, I'll take you. How does eight in the morning sound to you?"

"It sounds great," Einstein replied unenthusiastically.

He had planned to ask Greeley to g-mail him to the local authorities and call in the cavalry, but that was no longer an option. If the government was involved, he had no doubt that the local authorities would be as well. They would lock him up and throw away the key. He would disappear and never be heard from again, another casualty in the war for truth and justice. If he could get home, Einstein could get to his computer and send out a blog on *The Smoking Peashooter* about the dangerous plot being hatched in the middle of the Mojave. All he had to do was make it through the night. At this point there was only one person whom he could trust and that was himself. "If we're going to spend the night together," Einstein announced to the others, "I'd like to propose a few simple rules."

Einstein spent the next few minutes jotting something down in his notebook. He stopped briefly to review what he had written, then ripped out a single sheet of paper and handed it to Greeley. The ghost read it carefully, occasionally looking up to give Einstein a dirty look, and then passed the piece of paper to Roxie. "What's this?" she asked.

"The new house rules," Einstein answered.

"But it's my house!" Greeley muttered.

"Didn't you say that *mi casa es su casa*?" Einstein reminded him.

"Yes." Greeley sighed.

"Well, in my house we have rules."

"And I'll bet you ignore every single one of them," Greeley mumbled under his breath.

CHAPTER

22

Day Six — 9:36 P.M.

Curly was collecting the leftovers from dinner when he heard the familiar high-pitched squeals coming from the large room that was hidden behind the pantry. He walked over to a trash can and popped open the lid. The mashed horseflies that he had put in there yesterday had turned into a rancid-smelling pulp. The stench was overpowering, but that was what the recipe called for. Holding his breath, he dumped the leftovers into the pitch-black goop and mixed them in with a large wooden ladle. He filled a ten-gallon jug to the brim and replaced the lid to the trash can. With considerable effort, Curly lifted the jug, walked behind the pantry, and cautiously entered the secret room.

"Come and get it, boys," Curly shouted, dumping the mixture into a long trough through a vent in the doorway. He watched the five furry little creatures as they waddled over to the trough, tripping over their own cute little legs—all eight of them. The baby glokas were roughly the size of small sheepdogs and just as cuddly, with big black puppy-dog eyes. The difference was that each gloka had ten eyes in total, positioned equidistantly around the top of its head, providing a three-hundred-sixty-degree field of vision. It was almost impossible to sneak up on a gloka unless it was asleep, and even then, it slept with six eyes open.

As adorable as the babies were, Curly reminded himself, they were still potentially dangerous. All it would take was a hard rain and a leaky roof to instantly turn the cuddly infants into mature adults, and the adults were anything but cuddly. The adults were like land sharks with legs, fearless and efficient predators. The walls of the large room had been fitted with hurricane glass as an added precaution. It allowed Curly to monitor the glokas without having to go in the room. The door was made of heavy reinforced steel, with a slide lock. It seemed silly considering how docile the creatures were in their present state. Nonetheless, the precautions were necessary.

"Cute little guys, aren't they?" Big Al said, startling the cook.

"Until you add water," Curly replied. He looked at the infants and shook his head. "If you ask me, we'd be better off without them."

Big Al didn't disagree, but orders were orders. Glokas cocooned their prey and let them rot, eating them several weeks later. The spun metal cocoons were soft on the inside but impregnable, which made them perfect for transporting dangerous prisoners from location to location to ensure that they did not escape during prison transfers. They were also used to protect valuable cargo. Vampires, mummies, and werewolves all qualified on both counts. "Our customer wants the campers to be cocooned before transport," he replied. "If that's what he wants, that's exactly what he'll get."

"I know," Curly added before Big Al could finish the rest. "The customer is always right."

"Especially this customer," Big Al reminded the cook.

Bucky walked into the room and tapped on the window hard enough to startle the glokas. They stopped eating and tried to hide beneath the trough.

"Are the holding tanks complete?" Big Al asked Bucky.

"We're all set," he replied. "Six individual tanks for the glokas and three large holding pens for the campers, all built to specification. The unit was prefabricated."

They both glared at the cook. Thanks to Curly, they were short one gloka.

"What do you want me to do?" the cook asked. "Apologize again?" In addition to caring for the creatures, he had been assigned to pick up six males. The obvious difference in their coloring made it easy to tell a male from a female. The male's coat was dark green; the female's fur was the color of blood. It should have been easy, but Curly was completely color-blind.

When Big Al had discovered the furry red female mixed in with the males, he was furious. A mature female was four times the size of an adult male and far more dangerous, especially during mating season. He ordered Curly to destroy her immediately. The cook had taken her out to the desert and left her there to die, deciding to let one of the natural predators do his dirty work. After all, the female was just a helpless little baby. How was he to know that it was going to rain that night?

"You should have told me you were color-blind. Make one more mistake," Big Al warned the cook, "and we won't just be short a gloka, we'll be short a crew member. Am I making myself clear, Curly?"

"Clear as rain, boss," the cook replied.

"Has the truck been repaired?" Big Al asked Bucky, referring to the old pickup they had found rotting away in the barn.

"She won't win any races, but she runs."

Big Al nodded his approval. "Okay, let's get packed up in here and begin phase two of the operation. You two take the glokas to the barn and place them in separate holding tanks."

"Do you want 'em showered?" Curly asked.

"Not yet," Big Al replied. "That can wait until after we have moved all of the campers to the barn, right before we bag and tag them."

"The sooner the better," Bucky said. "We got twelve campers missing, including the Fleet kid. Someone or something is out there and we can't afford to lose anyone else."

They both looked at Curly again.

"The female *is* dead, isn't she?" Big Al asked the cook, his tone menacing.

Curly was smart enough to know better than to admit the truth, especially after Big Al had just threatened to kill him. "Of course she's dead, boss."

"Are you sure?" Big Al asked.

"Why should I lie?"

CHAPTER

23

Day Six — 11:06 P.M.

THE NEW HOUSE RULES

1. No loud shrieking permitted
   (after 10 P.M.).
2. No rattling of chains (or similar items).
3. No rearranging of cabin furniture
   without prior written permission.
4. No speaking in tongues or pig Latin.
5. No materializing out of thin air unless
   wearing pants.
6. No séances or conjuring of the dead
   (after 10 P.M.).
7. No levitating objects (especially me).
8. No sing-alongs or camp songs (ever).
9. No farting, especially with the
   windows shut.

As Roxie read the list, she couldn't help but giggle. A few seconds later, Greeley joined in and began to chuckle.

"Laugh all you want," Einstein said firmly, "but the rules are the rules."

"Who died and put you in charge?" Greeley asked. "Oops, I guess I did!"

The ghost laughed at his own joke and Roxie joined in.

All of a sudden, Einstein doubled over in pain. His belly cramped and felt like it was filled with lead. "You wouldn't have anything to eat around here, would you, Greeley?" Einstein groaned. His stomach made a gurgling noise, like gas bubbles rising from a tar pit. "I'm starving."

"It must be your lucky day, Houdini," the ghost replied. Greeley levitated a medium-sized brown box and dropped it at Einstein's feet. The parcel was stamped **FRAGILE** in at least six spots, but instructions had been completely ignored. The brown paper wrapping was torn and frayed. Three out of four corners had been completely crushed and were caked with sticky white goo. Greeley admired his work with a sense of pride. Tampering with the U.S. mail may be a federal offense, but mutilating it was a time-honored tradition. "I was going to give this to you earlier."

"Well, why didn't you?" Einstein asked, eyeing the box suspiciously.

"The truth is I forgot," Greeley replied. "You want to file a complaint or have a look-see?" He gave the pummeled package a good hard shake and it burst open at the seams. Einstein's eyes lit up as a bonanza of mutilated Twinkie cartons came tumbling out of the box like quarters from a winning slot machine. "Looks like you hit the jackpot, Houdini."

"You can say that again," Einstein said, ogling the Twinkies like a condemned prisoner about to eat his last meal. He picked one up off the floor and tore off the cellophane wrapper. Just as he was about to stuff it in his mouth, he hesitated and had second thoughts.

"Try one," he said to Greeley, tossing him a Twinkie. "It's delicious."

"No, thanks," the ghost said. "Junk food gives me gas, remember?"

"He thinks we tampered with his Twinkies," Roxie said, shaking her head. She reached out and took a bite of the Twinkie. "You happy now?"

He looked at Greeley.

"Okay, you win, but don't say I didn't warn you." The ghost stuffed the whole Twinkie in his mouth and smiled. "Hey, these things are pretty tasty! Let me have another one of those bad boys."

Einstein tossed one to the ghost and stared at the pile of Twinkies. Watching Roxie and Greeley eat only made matters worse. His stomach emitted a loud rumbling sound like a volcano about to erupt.

"We're not the bad guys, Fleet," Roxie said softly. "Believe it or not, we're on the same side. Let's have something to eat and try to relax for a while. Tomorrow is going to be a long day."

"No battle was ever won on an empty stomach, I suppose," Einstein conceded, grabbing a handful of Twinkies. "Let's eat!"

For the next thirty minutes they pounded down Twinkie after Twinkie. They talked and told jokes and ate their fill. Einstein felt the best that he had in days. He was certainly more rational. Greeley had rescued him from suffocating in his own sleeping bag. Even if she had been too late to prevent the attack the night before, Roxie had rescued him from the infirmary. They weren't the enemy. Slowly the tension disappeared and was replaced by a sense of camaraderie. Whatever they had to face, they would face as a team. After his sixth Twinkie, Greeley rolled over and fell asleep.

"That old coot has the right idea," Roxie said, yawning.

Einstein offered to take the first watch and let her get some rest as penance for his earlier outburst. "Get some sleep, comrade."

Before she could lay her head on the pillow, a mighty blast shook the room, followed by the sound of muffled laughter. Slowly, a foul stench permeated the room and lingered for what seemed like an eternity. "All right, who broke rule number nine?"

"It wasn't me," Einstein grumbled.

Another cannon exploded and echoed throughout the cabin. This shot was louder and more potent than the first.

"Don't say I didn't warn you." Greeley chuckled.

"Open the window," Einstein groaned. "It smells like something died in here."

"I resent that remark," the ghost replied.

"Everyone go to sleep," Roxie ordered as she buried her head under a pillow. "Like I said, tomorrow is going to be a long day."

Greeley launched another atomic bomb.

"It's going to be a long night too," Einstein moaned.

CHAPTER

24

Day Seven — 8:40 A.M.

The camp was quiet when Einstein awoke. Roxie was still asleep on the armchair next to him, but Greeley was nowhere to be found. He looked down at his watch to see the time and noticed that his knuckles were covered with tufts of brown fur. It hadn't been there when he'd gone to sleep the previous night, but it was certainly there now. There were thick patches of hair on his arms and legs as well. Einstein scanned the room to make sure that Roxie was still asleep and pulled open the front of his shorts to take a quick peek. Like most boys his age who had matured slowly, Einstein had prayed for puberty to arrive and end the merciless teasing of those who had sprouted hair in all the appropriate places. This wasn't exactly what he had in mind, but at least no one would make fun of him in gym class anymore.

"How they hangin', Houdini?" Greeley said, materializing next to the door.

"You're forty minutes late," Einstein replied, hiding his arms behind his back.

"Let me clue you in on a little something there, sonny. I work for the United States Postal Service. I don't have to show up anywhere on time." Greeley took a closer look at Einstein and made a clucking sound. "You need a shave, boy."

"Who needs a shave?" Roxie asked, rubbing the sleep from her eyes.

"Our little amigo," Greeley told her. "Looks like you were right."

Roxie examined his arms and legs, then pried open his top lip to take a peek at his teeth. They were yellow, but normal. Nothing a good brushing couldn't fix.

"Are you planning on buying me to race or to keep as a pet?" Einstein asked.

"Neither," she said, "but we do have a small problem. You're turning into a werewolf."

"You knew this was going to happen. That's why Greeley wanted to wait until morning to g-mail me home."

"I'm sorry, comrade," Roxie said softly. "I tried to get you out of the werewolf outfit as fast as I could, but I guess I wasn't fast enough."

"It was the salt tablets, wasn't it?"

Roxie nodded.

"SALT is an acronym for Synthetic Alteration of Life Transformation. I'm not sure exactly how it works, but the costumes play an integral role in the process. The tablets create a chemical reaction that causes a genetic mutation, combining your DNA with anything you are wearing. The result is a total transformation. In effect, if you're dressed as a werewolf, you become a werewolf."

"I don't feel like a werewolf," Einstein said.

"To achieve that requires encyclopedia-like knowledge of

the material," Roxie told him. "Every camper at Creepy Time has that in common, except for you. They were handpicked out of thousands of candidates for that reason. Between the countless hours spent watching reruns of the old horror flicks and reading vintage comic books, they have become experts on the material. That expertise creates the inner monster, so to speak. It's known as the ARMS effect."

"The what?" Einstein asked.

"Absorbed Reaction to Media Stimulation," Roxie replied, and then repeated the letters in the acronym slowly.

"So, let me see if I have this straight. I'm going to look like a werewolf, but I'm not going to act like one."

Roxie nodded again.

"This really sucks," Einstein groaned.

"Look at the bright side, Houdini," the ghost said, tugging on the boy's beard. "If you ever get out of here, you'll be able to go to an R-rated movie without being carded."

Einstein ignored him and tried to wrap his arms around the problem at hand. Every problem had a solution. All you needed to do was find it. "Toss me a Twinkie, will you, Greeley?" Einstein said. "I think better on a full stomach."

"Could I have one too?" the ghost asked, eyeing the pile.

"NO!" Roxie and Einstein shouted in unison.

Einstein paced across the room, eating the Twinkie while he pondered the problem. Why would anyone want to transform kids into monsters? It didn't make any sense. Big Al and his crew were either insane or being paid for their efforts, either of which was possible. If they were being paid, whoever was paying them was just as crazy as they were. Who in their right minds would release a plague upon the Earth? Suddenly, it dawned on him. "That's it!" he shouted. "It's a plague!"

"What are you talking about, Fleet?" Roxie asked.

"I've uncovered some conspiracies in my time, but this one takes the prize. It's absolutely brilliant. Why would you want to turn kids into monsters?"

Roxie and Greeley both shrugged.

"I'll tell you why in two words," Einstein said. "Fear and profit. Who stands to benefit the most if real live monsters were released into the general population?"

"Is it a multiple-choice question?" Greeley asked.

"The government and the big pharmaceutical companies would," Einstein shouted, pounding his fist on the chair. "The government benefits by getting increased budgets for military spending all across the board. The big pharmaceutical companies make out on both ends. They make money selling the government the salt tablets to create the disease and even more on the back end."

"What back end?" Roxie asked.

"They sell everyone who has been infected the antidote!" Einstein shouted.

"If there is an antidote," Roxie asked, "how do we get our hands on it?"

"That's the part I haven't worked out yet," Einstein replied as he headed for the door. "But I will."

"Where you going, Fleet?" Roxie asked.

"Out for some fresh air," he told her. He grabbed a fresh Twinkie and pointed a hairy finger at Greeley. "It's still a bit ripe in here, if you get my drift."

"Be careful out there," Roxie warned as he walked out the door. She waited until he was gone before saying another word. Roxie could feel the ghost's eyes burning a hole in the back of her head. "What is it?"

"Don't you think you should have told him the whole story?"

"What he doesn't know won't hurt him."

"I wouldn't be so sure of that," Greeley replied. "Look what happened to me."

CHAPTER

Day Seven — 10:32 A.M.

I've been thinking, honey," Shirley said to her husband.

Norman put down his newspaper and stifled a groan. Anytime his wife started a sentence with "I've been thinking, honey" it always signified trouble.

"Thinking about what, Shirley?"

"I think you should give Einstein a call to make sure he's all right."

"We discussed that," Norman said. "It's against the rules, remember?"

Shirley gave him the look. After twenty years of marriage, Norman knew that look all too well. He had one of two choices. He could either make the call or prepare himself for a full day of the silent treatment.

"What's the number?" He sighed.

Shirley read him the phone number listed in the brochure and he dialed. After twenty rings he hung up and dialed again with the same result. "Nothing," Norman grunted. "Not even a machine."

"Try the operator and see if the number is working."

Norman called the operator and waited. On the fifteenth

ring, he was connected to an automated service. After a half hour of inane questions and rerouting through the system, he finally reached a human being. She spoke in a monotone drone that made the automated voice seem positively cheerful. The operator attacked Norman with a barrage of silly questions as to why he couldn't follow instructions to get what information he needed from their state-of-the-art automated service. Only after she had succeeded in making Norman feel like a complete and total slacker did the operator relent and agree to see if the number was in service. Ten minutes later, she finally got back on the line and told him that not only was the number not in service, but that there was no Camp Creepy Time listed in Saugus or anywhere else in California for that matter. Before Norman could say another word, she called him a bonehead and then severed the connection.

"What did she say?" Shirley asked.

"She said that there isn't a listing for Creepy Time." He could see the look of terror on his wife's face and tried to rationalize the situation to calm her down. "Maybe they went on a field trip or something and forgot to leave on the answering machine."

"Maybe there was an accident!" Shirley screamed, working herself into a frenzy.

Norman shook his head. "If there was an accident, someone from the camp would contact us. It just doesn't make any sense."

"I told you that he wasn't ready for sleepaway camp," Shirley said. She put her face in her hands and started to sob.

"What are you talking about?" Norman replied defensively.

"You were the one who insisted that a summer of fresh air was just what the doctor ordered, remember?"

"Well," Shirley said, the tears beginning to flow. "Maybe I was wrong."

"Maybe we were both wrong," Norman replied.

"I want to see Einstein," Shirley said between sobs.

"Me too," Norman said as he rifled the drawer for his keys. "I'll go outside and fire up the Volvo while you get dressed. We're taking a road trip."

CHAPTER 26

Day Seven — 11:20 A.M.

T he code name for the plan is Operation Knuckleball," Einstein announced to the others. "Our mission is to locate the antidote. Our objective is to do so without getting killed. Any questions so far?"

Roxie raised her hand.

"Yes?" Einstein said, taking her question.

"How do you plan to do that?" she said. "Beside the fact that we are outnumbered and outgunned, we're not even certain there is an antidote, let alone how to find it."

"First of all, we need to even the odds," Einstein began. "To accomplish that, Greeley will have to possess one of them." He stared down the ghost. "You think you can handle that?"

"Piece of cake," Greeley snapped back. "It's all in the handbook."

"What handbook?" Einstein asked.

"*Possession for Dummies,*" Greeley quipped. "There's a whole chapter on the subject."

"Great," Einstein replied. "From there we move on to phase two of the operation and give camp management a taste of their own medicine."

"You mean to feed them salt tablets?" Roxie asked.

"That's exactly what I plan to do, Agent Rosenberg. Unless Nurse Knockwurst changes into a beauty queen, I'm sure that they will lead us directly to the antidote."

"We don't even know if the antidote exists," Roxie reminded him again.

"Second, we need to retain a positive attitude," Einstein replied, wagging his finger at Roxie. "Negative thoughts produce negative results."

"What about weapons, Fleet?"

"It's already been taken care of," Einstein replied. He picked up a burlap sack and dumped the contents on the floor. "How did we do, Greeley?"

"It's all there," he answered, grinning like a ghoul. "Rolls of lanyard material, Popsicle sticks, superglue, marbles, balloons, masking tape, and everything else you asked for, including every last salt tablet I could find."

"Good work, comrade." Einstein gave the old man a pat on the back. "My uncle is a bigwig at the post office. If we come out of this in one piece, I'll put in a good word for you."

"I'm permanently retired," the ghost replied, "but thanks anyway."

Einstein grabbed a handful of Popsicle sticks and went to work. He glued the sides of six sticks into a perfect hexagon, then filled the inner space with marbles and gently squeezed. In a few seconds the glue set and the sticks were locked in place. Einstein carefully wrapped layer upon layer of yellow lanyard around the sticks, stopping every so often to check the tension.

"What are you doing?" Roxie asked.

"These seemingly harmless items can be obtained almost anywhere, but in the hands of a master such as myself, they are actually the most lethal weapons that the L.A. public school system has to offer unless, of course, you happen to own an Uzi." Einstein loaded a marble into the makeshift peashooter and blew. The glass ball sailed across the room and hit the wall with a loud thud. "Think of it as a weapon of class destruction. Just a little something I picked up during my formative years in the jungle."

"You learned to make a peashooter out of Popsicle sticks in Africa?"

Einstein shook his head and laughed. "Junior high school. I was talking about the other jungle."

"Can you make me one of those?" Greeley asked.

Einstein reached into his pack and pulled out several peashooters. They were longer than the homemade version and looked a lot sturdier. "Here you go, Greeley. We use them as giveaways when you sign up for membership on the website. Take one and pass the rest out to your friends."

The ghost examined the weapon and smiled. On the side it read, *Compliments of The Smoking Peashooter*. "Thanks. I've always wanted one of these things."

"Why did you bother to make a peashooter if you already had an arsenal stashed in your pack?" Roxie asked.

"You know what they say about idle hands," Einstein replied. He looked down at his watch and checked the time. "Speaking of which, we'd better go to work."

Under Einstein's direction, Greeley dissolved several handfuls of salt tablets in a shallow bowl filled with water. The ghost stirred until they were whipped into a fluffy white paste and then injected the mixture into the center of a dozen Twinkies with a straw. Einstein inspected his work, resealed the cellophane, and then loaded the spiked Twinkies back into the twelve-pack carton. That done, Einstein poured more in the bowl and stirred the remaining salt tablets until they liquefied. The water was murky, but no worse than the water that came directly from the tap. He put a funnel into the mouth of one of the counselor's canteens and poured. Einstein marked a second canteen with an X and filled it to the brim with fresh tap water.

"Who's that for?" Roxie asked.

"It's for me," he replied. "It's hot as an oven in here. I'm thirsty."

Greeley picked up a balloon and began to inflate it. With a few twists and turns the balloon took on the shape of a toy poodle. "I love these things," he cackled.

"Me too," Einstein said. He selected a yellow balloon from the pile and went to work on the next item on his list. He carefully filled the balloon with superglue until it was about a quarter of the way full and made a whoopee cushion. Einstein had tested the item once on his vice principal's swivel chair and it had worked like a charm. In addition to receiving a three-day suspension from school, his parents had to cough up sixty bucks for a new pair of slacks.

"Peashooters and glue balloons." Roxie sighed. "How did I let you talk me into this?"

"This battle will be won with wits, not weapons," Einstein replied. "Besides, we have the element of surprise on our side."

125

"Not for long," Greeley said, pointing at the window.

Einstein peeked outside and saw the pickup truck. Bucky and Curly were headed straight for the cottage.

"Any other bright ideas, General?" Roxie asked.

"Just one," Einstein whispered. "Everybody hide!"

CHAPTER 27

Day Seven — 11:45 A.M.

Curly watched as Bucky drove off, leaving a trail of dust behind. They had flipped a coin to see who would check out the cottage and who would go to the infirmary to help Nurse Knockwurst load the mummies into the pickup. Curly won the toss and selected the easier of the two assignments. The cook had expected to find the cottage deserted, but he was wrong. From the pile of contraband sitting in the center of the room, it was obvious that someone had been here. Judging by the collection of crumpled cellophane wrappers strewn about the floor, that someone had to be Einstein. He scanned the room for any sign of the boy. Taking no chances, Curly pulled a flat metallic object out of his pocket and held it in front of him. "This here is a Gregorian Model 3-P6 Plasma Blaster, one of the deadliest weapons ever made," he shouted. "It has three settings: stun, sting, and kill."

"What is it set on right now?" Einstein asked from his hiding spot. Due to his size, he was only able to squeeze about halfway under the sagging cot, leaving the backside of his body completely exposed. All things considered, it was a rather embarrassing position.

"It's set on sting and pointed right at your rear." Curly laughed, preparing to fire. "I'm going to use your tush for target practice."

Someone cackled at the remark, but it wasn't Einstein. The laughter was coming from the ceiling, directly above the spot on which he was standing. Curly looked up and saw nothing. "Come down from there or I'll shoot!"

"Go ahead and blast away," Greeley said, materializing right next to him. The ghost moved closer until he and Curly were standing nose to nose. "I'll make it easy for you."

Curly squeezed off a few rounds, but none of them hit the mark. Instead, they passed right through Greeley and hit the wall, splintering apart large chunks of wood in the process. The blood drained from Curly's face. He backed up and continued to fire as Greeley walked toward him. Finally, the cook bumped into an easy chair and could not back up any farther.

"Have a seat, sonny," Greeley said, giving Curly a push. The yellow seat cushion exploded with a loud pop, releasing the glue. Curly tried to stand up, but to no avail. His rear end was stuck to the chair.

"I'll take that," Roxie said, standing directly behind him. She reached over and grabbed the blaster out of Curly's hand. Roxie examined the weapon for any sign of superglue that may have splattered when the balloon exploded. Satisfied that the blaster was in perfect working order, she switched on the safety and tucked it into the top of her pants.

"Where did you learn to handle a blaster?" Curly asked, eyeing Roxie up and down. There were only two female campers enrolled at Creepy Time—or at least there used to be, before they disappeared—and this girl wasn't one of them.

"Sit there and keep quiet," Roxie ordered. She turned around to let Einstein know that the coast was clear. "You can come out now, Fleet. Your plan worked like a charm."

"A little help would be appreciated, comrade," Einstein grunted as he tried to pry himself free. "I seem to be stuck."

Greeley levitated the cot a couple of feet off the floor and Einstein backed out from his hidey-hole. He picked himself up and dusted the soot from his shirt. He noticed the smirk on Curly's face. "What's so funny?"

"You're looking a little furrier than the last time I saw you," Curly snickered. "Let's hear a good howl!"

"You want to hear me howl?" Einstein said. "Fix some lunch."

Roxie flipped the setting on the ray gun from stun to kill and pointed it at the cook. "Where's the antidote to the salt tablets?"

"I don't know what you're talking about," the cook said nervously.

Roxie fired a shot above his head and blew a hole in the wall.

"I don't know!" Curly screamed.

"You think he's telling the truth?" Einstein whispered in Roxie's ear.

Roxie nodded.

"Looks like it's your turn at bat," Einstein said to Greeley. Before Curly could say boo, the ghost entered his body. The cook's eyes went blank. He tried to speak but could not seem to form words. This was the part of the plan that no one was sure would work. The ghost was certainly capable of possession, but the problem was that he had never done it before. It was unexplored territory, in more ways than one.

"You in there, Greeley?" Einstein asked.

"It ain't Whistler's mother," the ghost replied.

"How do you feel?"

"Claustrophobic," he replied. "It's crowded in here. Maybe I should have possessed Nurse Knockwurst instead."

"It's too late for that," Roxie said. The red truck pulled up next to the cottage and honked the horn. The flatbed was loaded with mummies. She handed the ghost the canteen and the carton of spiked Twinkies. "It's showtime, Greeley."

"Good luck, comrade," Einstein said as the ghost waddled toward the door, the chair still attached to his rear.

"I'm not your comrade," Curly said, sneering at Einstein. Suddenly, the cook slapped himself across the face and apologized.

"Ignore him, Houdini," the ghost replied. "He's a jerk."

Greeley and Curly seemed to be wrestling for control of the cook's body. Roxie and Einstein watched them walk toward the truck, praying that Greeley could dominate Curly long enough for the plan to have a chance to work.

"What happened to you?" Bucky shouted, doing his best not to laugh.

"The kid booby-trapped the place and left a glue bomb on the chair," Greeley replied. He looked down at the carton he was holding. "I got even and stole the last of his Twinkies."

"We could use them for bait," Nurse Knockwurst suggested.

"Let's eat them instead," Greeley replied. "It will drive the kid nuts."

Bucky pointed at the chair and laughed. "You need some help with that?"

"All I can get, sonny," Greeley replied, catching his mistake immediately. He noticed the sideways glance that Bucky shot at the nurse.

Nurse Knockwurst locked her arms around Curly's neck while Bucky pulled on his legs.

"Are you two crazy?" Curly screamed, his pain forcing Greeley out.

"You want help or not?" Bucky grunted, pulling harder. "Make up your mind."

Nurse Knockwurst didn't wait for a reply. She tightened the choke hold around the cook's neck and pulled with all her might. Bucky grabbed hold of the chair and pulled in the opposite direction. Curly felt like he was being stretched on the rack. He could feel the ligaments in his body stretching and cried out in pain. Bucky and Nurse Knockwurst took that as a good sign that they were making progress and pulled even harder. A sharp snapping sound sent Curly into a tizzy. "Was that my neck or my legs?"

"It was your pants," Nurse Knockwurst informed him. He noticed that she was staring.

"I see London. I see France. I see Curly's underpants."

Greeley took control and covered Curly's rear end with the

box of Twinkies. It was one thing to get caught with your pants down, but it was another to be caught wearing heart-covered silk boxers. Even the ghost was embarrassed for the cook.

"Let's get these campers to the barn before they come to and cause trouble," Bucky said as he followed Curly to the truck. "After we load them and the others, we have less than twenty-four hours and we're out of here. You ask me, it's not a moment too soon," he whispered, casting a glance at Nurse Knockwurst.

"I'll whip up something special for dinner to celebrate," Greeley replied.

"How about a nice worm potpie?" Bucky asked as he got in the truck. He looked at Curly and laughed. "By the way, I forgot to tell you something."

"What's that?"

"Love your undies."

CHAPTER 28

Day Seven — 1:59 P.M.

"The camp should be around here somewhere," Norman said, pointing at the map. He slammed on the brakes of his dust-covered Volvo and came to an abrupt halt in the middle of the highway. There was nothing but empty desert for as far as the eye could see. Norman picked up the map and studied it again, for the fifth time in the last fifteen minutes. "Either these directions stink or I copied down the address wrong."

"Why can't you just admit that you're lost?" Shirley Fleet asked. After three hours on the road, her nerves were starting to fray.

"I'm not lost," Norman grumbled.

"You're kidding me, right?" Shirley rolled her eyes to emphasize the point. "Why don't you ask someone for directions?"

"Who would you like me to ask?" Norman replied, his tone thick with sarcasm. "The cactus over there?"

Shirley gave him the look.

"Hello, Mr. Cactus," Norman shouted out the window. "How do I find Camp Creepy Time? You don't know? Well, thanks anyway. Wait a minute, there's a scorpion! Maybe he knows."

"Why don't you just go back to the gas station that we

passed a few miles ago and ask them for directions?" Shirley snapped at her husband. "Would you please roll up your window while you're at it? It's like an oven in here."

"Fine," Norman said as he rolled up the window. He made a U-turn and headed back in the opposite direction. "We need to get some gas anyway."

They drove the three miles back to the filling station without saying another word to each other. Norman pulled the Volvo up to the pump as a freckle-faced teenager approached the vehicle.

"What will it be, mister?" the grease monkey asked as he wiped the sweat from his brow with a dirty rag, leaving a black oily trail across his forehead.

"I need gas and directions," Norman replied. He handed the map to the gas attendant and pointed to the address. "We're looking for Creepy Time."

The boy looked at the map and scratched his head.

"It's a summer camp," Shirley added.

"Never heard of it," he replied, "but you came to the right place." He pointed to the convenience store behind the gas station. The numbers stenciled across the top of the door were the same as those on the map. "You sure about that address?"

"No, not entirely," Norman replied, wishing he had not left the brochure behind. He could feel his wife's staring eyes burning a hole in the back of his head. "Is there anyone else around who may know where to find the camp?"

"You can go talk to old man Warner if you want." The boy shrugged. "He owns the store."

"Fill her up and check the oil," Norman said. "We'll be right back."

The convenience store was cluttered with the normal array of items one would expect to find and some that one would not. Shirley noticed a baby's rattle made from the tail end of a real rattlesnake. She picked it up and gave it a good shake, scaring Norman half to death.

"If you break it, you buy it." The warning came from the man standing behind the counter, which was just as cluttered as the rest of the store. The man was so short that all Norman could see was the top of his balding head peeking over the counter.

"Are you Mr. Warner?" Norman asked.

"I'm Warner," the old man replied. "What's it to you?"

"We're lost and that nice young man pumping our gas thought you may be able to help," Shirley explained. "Do you know how to get to a camp called Creepy Time?"

"Never heard of it," the old man replied.

"Are there any other summer camps around here?" Norman asked, deciding to take a different approach.

Warner scratched his head and gave the matter some thought, then snapped his bony fingers together. "Come to think of it, there was a camp—but I can't remember the name. An old-timer named Greeley used to run the place."

Norman and Shirley exchanged a smile at the mention of Greeley's name. At last they were getting somewhere.

"What's so funny?" Warner asked.

"I'm sorry," Norman replied. "We're just relieved. Our

son mentioned Greeley in one of his letters. Is he a friend of yours?"

Now it was Warner's turn to laugh. "I called him an old-timer, because that's what he was when I opened this place."

"Was?" Shirley asked.

"Greeley died over forty years ago," Warner explained. "Big scandal as I recall. Lot of campers went missing. The police suspected Greeley was involved and tried to get to the bottom of it, but they never got very far. A couple of years after the incident, he died. The case was closed and the campers were never found."

Norman and Shirley stared at each other in a state of shock. Norman tried to say something, but was unable to speak.

"What's wrong?" the old man asked. "You two look pale as a ghost."

The Fleets flew out of the store without bothering to say good-bye and ran as fast as they could toward their car.

"Einstein was telling the truth and we didn't believe him!" Shirley sobbed, trying to keep up with Norman. "What are we going to do?"

"I'll tell you what we're going to do," Norman shouted back. "We're going to find the nearest town and talk to the police."

As soon as they were in the car, Shirley picked up the map. Norman grabbed it and crumpled it into a ball. "Just ask the kid for directions," he said as he turned over the ignition.

"How far to the sheriff's office?" Shirley screamed out the window.

"You have to go to Saugus," the boy replied. "Take a right

out of the station and keep going straight. It's about thirty miles down the road."

Norman peeled out of the station, leaving a trail of burning rubber behind as he fishtailed out of the driveway and onto the main road.

"Hey, mister!" the grease monkey shouted at the rear end of the Volvo. "You forgot to pay for the gas!"

CHAPTER

Day Seven — 2:17 P.M.

All of the campers had been moved to the barn and imprisoned in three separate cages. The cages were cramped and uncomfortable, with barely enough room to move. The campers complained bitterly. Bucky and Nurse Knockwurst stood in front of the vampire cage, discussing which group to cocoon first. All three groups volunteered. Anything was better than being packed like a can of sardines, especially given the heat. Greeley was inside Curly's body, listening to every word, while Roxie and Einstein watched from a safe distance.

"What *are* those things?" Einstein asked.

"Glokas," Roxie whispered.

The glokas were hopping up and down, confined in their own separate cages. As soon as they saw Curly, the five furry creatures clambered to the front of the reinforced Plexiglas and began to beg for food. They stood on their back legs, yelping like little puppy dogs.

"Cute little guys, aren't they?" Einstein whispered to Roxie.

"Not for long," she replied as Nurse Knockwurst gave Curly the order to turn on the shower.

"Which button is it?" Greeley asked, staring at the remote.

He may have possessed Curly's mind and body, but he didn't possess his knowledge. Greeley had no idea how to work this contraption. There were literally dozens of different buttons on the device, all of them labeled in an alien language that was impossible to decipher.

"It's the red one, you idiot!" Nurse Knockwurst shouted. "The green button activates the protective field around the cages. What's wrong with you, Curly?"

"I'm not myself today," Greeley cackled as he pushed the red button.

Water poured down into the cages like rain, drenching the furry little babies. Their transformation from infants to adults was as quick as it was startling. The eight stubby legs hidden beneath their long shaggy coats sprouted instantaneously, growing longer and more muscular. Their soft fur was replaced with thick slimy scales, like an oily coat of armor. All ten of their large button eyes exploded at once. Immediately they were replaced with ten black and bulbous new eyes that resembled giant Tootsie Pops attached to the tips of octopus-like tentacles. Einstein felt a chill run down his spine as two large metallic fangs emerged amid several rows of sharp teeth. The adult glokas opened their mouths and roared, the sound echoing through the barn like thunder.

"Yikes!" Einstein gasped.

"You should see the females." Roxie waved her arms at Greeley and tried to get his attention, but he was facing the other direction and couldn't see her. "I could use some help here, Fleet."

Einstein took out his peashooter and loaded it with a marble. He took a deep breath and aimed. The marble sailed across the barn and hit Greeley in the butt. The ghost turned around and glared at Einstein. When he did, Roxie motioned for him to come closer. Greeley started toward them, but didn't get very far.

"Where do you think you're going?" Bucky shouted.

"Nature calls," Greeley replied without turning around, his eyes glued to Roxie.

"Push the yellow button," she mouthed silently.

"Your mind turn into Jell-O?" Bucky said, pointing at the glokas. "You forgot to turn on the force field."

"Did you say yellow?" Greeley asked, turning around.

"Are you crazy, fool?" Bucky replied, shaking his head. "You want to bring down the ship? Push the green one."

Greeley pushed the yellow button instead. "Oops."

A spaceship came crashing down through the roof. A giant dust cloud filled the barn. When it cleared, the ship was sitting in the exact spot where the six cages had been moments before, and the glokas were gone. All that remained was a solitary Tootsie Pop eye, peeking out from beneath the hull of the ship.

Einstein's jaw dropped at the sight of the spaceship. He stared at Roxie in disbelief. "You and I need to have a little talk," he whispered.

"Not here," Roxie said. "Let's go back to the cottage."

"What about Greeley?" Einstein asked.

"Don't worry about Greeley," Roxie replied. "They can't do anything to him that they haven't done already."

CHAPTER

30

Day Seven — 2:43 P.M.

Chief Chester had heard more than his share of far-fetched stories, but this one was a real doozy. The portly policeman had chosen the desert community because of its peaceful nature, far removed from the hustle and bustle of big-city life and big-city crazies. Now two of those crazies were sitting five feet across from his desk and refused to budge. The chief opened his desk drawer and fished out a doughnut. It may be his job to listen to this drivel, but it didn't mean that he had to starve to death while doing it. "How did you hear about this alleged camp?"

"We got a brochure in the mail," Norman replied.

"Can I see it?" the chief asked.

Shirley looked at her husband and rolled her eyes. "He left it at home."

Chief Chester leaned back in his swivel chair and smiled.

"I know the whole thing sounds crazy," Norman sighed.

"You think?" the chief replied. He took a large bite out of the jelly doughnut and then wiped his mouth clean with his sleeve. "Do you want to file a missing persons report?"

"Haven't you been listening to a word of this?" Shirley screamed at the chief. "Our son has been kidnapped! He's probably rotting in a hole somewhere while you sit on your rump eating that doughnut."

"Are you folks on drugs?"

Norman took a deep breath and tried to remain calm. "We're not on drugs or any type of medication. We're just concerned parents, trying to find our son. He wrote to tell us that he was in trouble, but we didn't listen. If you don't believe me, read his last letter." He handed the white envelope to Chief Chester.

The chief noticed that it did not have a stamp, confirming his suspicion that this was some type of prank. Either the kid was at home or the Fleets had penned it themselves. It was possible that the boy didn't even exist. Nonetheless, he went through the motions and read the letter inside. Taking no chances, he held the paper in one hand and fingered the gun in his holster with the other and started to read. The letter was even crazier than the two people sitting in his office, but if nothing else, at least it was good for a chuckle. He handed the letter back to Shirley, leaned back in his seat, and took another bite of his doughnut.

"Well, what do you think now?" Norman asked.

"Real chip off the old block, isn't he?" the chief replied through a mouthful of jelly. "Have you folks ever considered family counseling?"

"We're not crazy!" Norman shouted. "Just call the old guy out at the convenience store. He knows all about Greeley and Sleepy Time."

"Listen, folks," the chief began, eyeballing the Fleets like a couple of small-time criminals in a police lineup. "Saugus may be a small town and we may be just a bunch of redneck yahoos to you, but we know a big-city prank when we see one. Now, if you've had your fun, I'd like to get home and watch a rerun of *The Dukes of Hazard* with the rest of the rubes."

Before Norman could say another word, the phone rang. Chief Chester leaned over and picked it up. "Speak of the devil," he said, covering the mouthpiece. "It's Jim Warner."

As the chief spoke to the man who owned the convenience store, Norman whispered to his wife. "At last we're getting somewhere," he said with confidence.

After a brief conversation, Chief Chester hung up the phone and pulled out his gun. "You're both under arrest."

"What for?" Norman growled at the cop.

"They may be giving away free gas in the city," the chief replied calmly, "but around these parts we expect folks to pay for it. Get up against the wall and assume the position."

Five minutes later, the Fleets found themselves in a small but private cell, spending the night in jail courtesy of one angry redneck sheriff. Shirley was curled up on a cot in the fetal position, crying like a baby. Norman was pacing back and forth across the cell like a caged tiger. "Just wait until I get my lawyer on the phone. Just you wait!"

"Just shut up, Norman!" Shirley wailed.

143

CHAPTER 31

Day Seven — 3:07 P.M.

We're being abducted by aliens and sold to an intergalactic monster zoo?" Einstein gasped, staring at Roxie in disbelief. He repeated the information over and over again, as if doing so would make it less true, then bent over and placed his hands on his knees. "I think I'm going to be sick."

According to Roxie, Big Al and the others were extraterrestrial gangsters masquerading as counselors, with rap sheets a mile long. They worked for Mucho Fahn, an intergalactic wheeler-dealer who had built a criminal empire that spanned two galaxies. No one had ever seen Mucho Fahn and very little was known about him, but his ruthlessness was legendary. Roxie was part of a task force that had been specially commissioned to track Mucho Fahn down and bring him to justice. IMPS had been after him and his gang for years. They had followed his trail from one planet to the next, with the same result. Mucho Fahn remained one step ahead of them every step of the way.

"You're telling me that our government has the ability to track criminals from one planet to another?" Einstein snickered. "We can barely get a space probe to Mars."

"IMPS isn't part of *your* government," Roxie replied. "It's extraterrestrial."

"Extraterrestrial?" Einstein took the news like a sucker punch to the belly. If IMPS was alien, it stood to reason that all of the agents that worked for the organization were too. "You're joking, right?"

Roxie shook her head.

"You're an alien?" Einstein uttered in disbelief.

"I wanted to tell you, but I thought you'd freak out."

"Freak out?" he mumbled to himself. Einstein's breathing grew rapid and labored. He began to hyperventilate. "I've got two friends in the world—one lives in another dimension and the other lives in another galaxy. Why would I freak out?"

"I'm sorry," Roxie said softly. "I should have told you sooner. This is a lot to absorb all at one time."

It was hard to tell if Einstein was listening. He muttered "I can't believe you're an alien" several times and keeled over, falling face-first onto the floor.

Roxie bent over and cradled his head in her arms. She picked up the canteen and splashed some fresh water on his face. A few minutes later, Einstein opened his eyes.

"What happened?" he asked, rubbing his head.

"You fainted," she said. Roxie handed him the canteen and instructed him to take a couple of short sips. Einstein eyed her suspiciously. "Relax, Fleet. I'm not going to hurt you."

"I can't believe you're an alien," he repeated.

"I'm a friend," Roxie replied. "If we're going to survive this, we're going to have to trust each other and work as a team."

Einstein knew that she was right. He needed Roxie, human

or not. On his own, Einstein didn't stand a chance. He took a long swig from the canteen.

"Where is this zoo?" Einstein asked.

"No one knows except for Mucho Fahn," explained Roxie. "The location is a well-guarded secret. As an added precaution, it's rumored that he moves the zoo constantly. Even the paying guests don't know the location until the very last minute. IMPS tried to infiltrate his operation once. Two of our agents posed as guests. Neither of them was ever heard from again. Once Big Al is ready to go, he will make contact and Mucho Fahn will provide him with the coordinates for the current location. After that, the ship will transport the campers through a wormhole to the zoo."

"A wormhole?" he repeated. In theory, a wormhole was a way to travel through vast distances of space without the passage of time. The idea of being jettisoned through millions of miles of space at the speed of light made his stomach roll. "I hope they have barf bags aboard."

"If it makes you feel any better, you were partially right about the involvement of both the government and several major conglomerates."

"Excuse me?"

"After the crash at Roswell, the government made a deal to trade advanced alien technology in exchange for the right to abduct a limited number of human beings. The government received detailed plans that allowed them to build stealth fighters, cloaking devices, cell phones, plasma televisions, and a whole slew of other worthless things. All of this stuff is primitive by alien standards, but the right to abduct humans was priceless to Mucho Fahn."

"Back up for a second," Einstein said. "Are you saying that the government made a deal with an intergalactic criminal?"

"They didn't know that Mucho Fahn was a criminal," Roxie replied. "They thought that he represented a peaceful federation of alien planets. The truth of the matter is that travel to this planet was banned over a thousand years ago. Alien tourists used to love to come here and party. Unfortunately, it got out of hand and was stopped after a few bad apples pretended they were gods and ruined it for everyone."

Einstein took his notebook out and opened it. "Were the humans used like lab rats for medical experiments or sold as slaves to work on third-world planets?" Einstein asked, jotting down a few notes. "Interested bloggers are dying to know."

"Neither," Roxie replied. "The humans are placed on exhibition in his zoo. Mucho Fahn charges a fortune for the cost of admission, which doesn't even include the tickets for the rides. Since he has a captive audience, he's able to demand outrageous prices for the rooms in the hotel. The concession stands are an even bigger rip-off. And the licensing of merchandise is a real gold mine. Mucho has made a fortune. Think about it, Fleet. How much would you pay to see a zoo full of aliens?"

"After they were turned into monsters?"

Roxie shook her head.

"Why would anyone be interested in seeing a zoo filled with human beings?" Einstein asked. "I thought you said it was a monster zoo."

"It is," Roxie replied. "Most intergalactic life-forms think humans are hideous-looking creatures."

"Do you think we're hideous?" he asked, wondering what was under her costume. Einstein hoped that she didn't look like one of the crab creatures from the *Predator* movies. "Take off that getup and let's see what you look like."

"I'm not taking off anything," Roxie said in a huff.

"I knew it!" he screamed. "You're a crab creature!"

"The universe is infinite," Roxie replied. "Have you ever considered the possibility that there are other life-forms that look just like you?"

"Are you one of them?" he asked Roxie.

"Yes."

A sense of relief washed over Einstein. His camp crush may be an alien, but at least she was cute. "What about Big Al and the others?"

Roxie shook her head. "Trust me, Fleet. You don't want to know."

"I'm still confused about one thing," Einstein said, thinking out loud. "Why would Mucho Fahn be interested in werewolves, mummies, and vampires, especially the ones that were from the old sci-fi flicks of the fifties?"

"To tell you the truth, I'm confused too," she admitted. "It's the first time that I know of that this has ever happened. The salt tablets are a new twist, but it explains why they came to Earth."

"I'm lost again," Einstein confessed.

"If you fed the salt tablets to any life-form and placed them in a mummy suit, you'd end up with a replication of a mummy.

But it would just be a replication and no more. The ARMS effect wouldn't be a factor."

"Why not?"

"Those old black-and-white movies and the characters in them are unique to your planet. Your species is the only life-form in the known universe that is completely immersed in media. As a result of this constant bombardment, the lines between fact and fiction have blurred. More than likely, the ARMS effect wouldn't work anywhere else but Earth."

Einstein considered what Roxie had said and carefully digested the information. "That's a big problem," he said with a sigh. "If Mucho Fahn wants more monsters, he'll just come back to Earth and take them. Hundreds of others will be transformed, abducted, and never heard from again. We have to stop him."

"Unfortunately, we have a more immediate problem," Roxie replied. "If we don't find the antidote and turn the campers back into normal kids, they are going to be no worse off in the zoo than they will be here on Earth."

"You're right." Einstein frowned. "We have to find the antidote somehow, but it's going to take time."

"Losing the glokas was a setback for them," Roxie told him. "The campers will have to be loaded for transport manually. That ought to buy us some time."

"How much time?" Einstein asked.

"Less than twenty-four hours."

CHAPTER

Day Seven — 3:28 P.M.

Oops?" Bucky repeated, staring at Curly in disbelief.

"You said to push the yellow button," Greeley replied, playing innocent. "So I pushed it. What's the problem?"

"You just killed all of the glokas! That's the problem, you idiot!" Bucky looked at the body parts splattered all over the barn and sighed. "When Big Al finds out, he's going to rip us limb from limb."

"Not necessarily," Nurse Knockwurst mumbled. "Especially if he doesn't know."

"Are you suggesting that we lie to him?" Bucky asked.

"That's exactly what I'm suggesting," the nurse replied. "We'll have to pack up the campers and load them by hand."

"That will take hours," Bucky moaned.

"Let's weigh our options," Nurse Knockwurst growled. "We can either spend a few hours doing manual labor or tell Big Al and be dead for the rest of our lives. Which option would you prefer?"

"The first one," Bucky admitted.

"Then we better get started." She took out her blaster and set it on stun. Bucky followed suit and did the same. Greeley stood there and looked lost. "Now what?" Nurse Knock-wurst sighed.

"I seem to have misplaced my blaster," Greeley muttered. "You got a spare?"

"Get the wheelbarrow and all the tape you can haul," she ordered, pointing at a stack of boxes on the other side of the barn. "Six cases of electrician's tape and twelve cases of painter's tape ought to do the trick."

Greeley walked across the barn to fetch the wheelbarrow as Nurse Knockwurst and Curly blasted away. One by one, the werewolves and mummies were stunned and rendered unconscious. The vampires, however, proved more difficult targets. Some turned into bats and attempted to escape, but the bars on the cage were too narrow. Others used their supernatural powers to move from one side of the cage to the other, faster than the eye could follow. They would disappear for a moment and reappear in a new location, easily dodging the blasters.

"Missed me again, you ugly vitch," Vinnie taunted from the back of the cage. She fired another shot and missed once again. The nurse could hear him laughing. He reappeared sitting cross-legged at the front of the cage and smiled at her. "Vant to go for two out of three?"

"Stand still," Nurse Knockwurst demanded. She was dripping in sweat and her bun was wilting from the heat. The nurse's costume was starting to stretch in the heat. The effect was shocking. Her alien half was starting to show and it wasn't a pretty sight. "I'm taking off this costume," she shouted at Bucky. "I can't breathe."

"Me too," Bucky replied. "It will be easier to work without it."

Greeley panicked. The salt tablets wouldn't work on them if they took off their costumes. And they would expect him to do the same. "Big Al said that we shouldn't expose ourselves in public," he said, snickering at his own joke.

"Big Al isn't here, is he?" Bucky replied.

"Suit yourself," Greeley said, "but don't say I didn't warn you."

"You got the energy to chase down the rest of the vampires, then go ahead and do it," Bucky challenged. "This whole mess is your fault in the first place."

"Who wants to see Nurse Knockwurst and Bucky get naked?" Greeley shouted. A loud chorus of groans echoed through the cage. "I'll give you ten seconds to show yourselves or they start to strip!"

The vampires materialized one by one. Vinnie was the last to appear. "And you call us monsters?" he hissed. "Vat are you vaiting for? Hurry up and shoot!"

Bucky and Nurse Knockwurst blasted away at the vampires and dragged them out of the cage. They piled them next to the wheelbarrow as Greeley fumbled with the remote. "Which one opens the hatch again?" he asked.

Nurse Knockwurst grabbed the remote out of his hand and pressed the button that released the door to the ship. It slowly descended until it hit the barn floor. "What are *you* waiting for?" she shouted at the others. "A written invitation? They're not going to load themselves into the pods. Let's get them bagged and tagged. Daylight is wasting, gentlemen."

Bucky helped Curly throw a couple of the werewolves into the wheelbarrow and followed Nurse Knockwurst onto the ship. "You better make something real special for dinner tonight, Curly," Bucky said, poking the cook in the chest. "Real special."

"That's just what I had in mind."

CHAPTER

33

Day Seven — 7:05 P.M.

Big Al was smiling and cordial, which had the rest of his crew on edge. He rarely smiled. When he did, it usually meant he was either getting ready to eat or getting ready to kill someone. The crew sat silently at the dinner table as Curly scurried about the pantry, gathering up dinner, watching Big Al and hoping he was hungry.

"You're in a good mood tonight," Nurse Knockwurst said, finally breaking the silence. "Why?"

"Why not?" Big Al replied cheerfully. "By this time tomorrow, the mission will be complete and we'll be rich beyond our wildest dreams. So, what's for dinner, Curly? I'm starving! Word is going around that you have something special planned."

Bucky and Knockwurst breathed a sigh of relief.

"Chili and beans," Greeley replied as he opened a can and poured the contents into the pot. He added some water from the canteen spiked with salt tablets and stirred it in with a large wooden spoon. "Aged to perfection. It's a vintage 1962."

"Where on Earth did you find those?" Big Al asked, eyeing the cans on the countertop. The cans were covered with rust. The labels were peeling off and faded.

"They were in the pantry," Greeley replied. "Been there for years, I suppose. You know the old saying—finders keepers, losers weepers."

"I've never heard that one before," Big Al replied. "It's an interesting concept."

"It's not a concept," Greeley said. "It's just an old saying."

"Like nine Mongorian dragon heads are better than one," Big Al said.

"Exactly," the ghost replied.

Bucky walked over to the counter, curious to see what was in the other bowl. It was filled to the brim with plump white insects. He popped one in his mouth and chewed. "I don't know what this is, but it's sure tasty!"

"That's a maggot. It's my secret ingredient," Greeley said as he grabbed a handful and tossed them in the pot.

"Can I try one?" Nurse Knockwurst asked, smacking her lips.

She reached out and Greeley whacked her across the knuckles with the wooden spoon. "Not before dinner. You don't want to ruin your appetite."

Greeley opened four more cans of stale chili that were a good forty years past their prime and scooped them one by one into the pot. He tried his best not to breathe in the aroma. It smelled rancid, even to a dead man. The ghost served Bucky first and then Nurse Knockwurst. They dove in without waiting for Big Al to be served.

Bucky noticed that Big Al was staring. "Sorry, boss."

"Don't be ridiculous," Big Al replied. "Eat up, before it gets cold."

"You sure?" Bucky asked.

Big Al nodded and watched them eat while he waited for the cook to prepare his plate. "After dinner, we're going to torch the whole camp," he said, smiling at Curly. "We can roast a few marshmallows over a burning campfire, if you get my drift."

"Why bother burning down the place?" Bucky asked. "It's already rotting. In a few years the desert will finish the job."

"I don't want to leave any evidence behind this time," Big Al replied. "Besides, the place is an eyesore. Think of it as a service to a community that has given us back so much in return."

The comment infuriated the ghost. No one was going to burn down the house that Greeley built, especially if he had something to say about it. He swatted Big Al on the top of his head with the chili-covered wooden spoon.

"What did you do that for?" Big Al asked, glaring at him.

"Sorry 'bout that. I thought I saw a maggot crawling in your hair. It must have gone over the bowl." Without any further warning, he swatted Big Al again. "There it is again. I think I got it that time."

Big Al wiped the chili splatter off his forehead with a napkin as Greeley topped Big Al's serving of chili off with the left-over maggots. Greeley placed the scalding hot bowl of chili in front of Big Al and "accidentally" pushed it on his lap. The alien screamed in pain. Greeley apologized to Big Al profusely and went to get him another bowl. "I don't know what's got into me today," Greeley said, holding back a snicker.

"I do, Greeley," Big Al replied. He stood up and drew his blaster. The others followed his lead. "Release Curly's body immediately."

"Possession is nine tenths of the law," Greeley said.

"Exorcism is the other tenth," Big Al growled, "and I hope you hate every minute of it." He turned to his crew and gave the order to fire.

"Let him have it, boys!" Nurse Knockwurst screamed. They simultaneously fired at Curly with their blasters set on stun. The three blue beams of light crossed and formed one powerful beam. Curly's hair stood on end and caught on fire. His eyes glazed over and he fell to his knees. The alien was near death when Greeley emerged from his body. They reset their blasters to kill and continued to fire at the ghost.

"I'm melting," Greeley whined.

"Good job, everyone," Big Al said.

"How did you figure it out?" Bucky asked as he watched the ghost's body fade.

"A Mongorian dragon has three heads, not nine. Any fool knows that, except for an old human fool," Big Al replied as he took another shot at Greeley. He stared at the ghost with venom in his eyes. "And this time stay dead. I'm getting tired of killing you!"

Greeley made a final obscene gesture at Big Al and disappeared.

The nurse went over to check on Curly. A cloud of steam was emanating from his body. She knelt down to see if he had a pulse. It was faint, but it was there.

"How is he?" Big Al asked.

"He'll live." She dumped what water remained in the canteen over his body to cool him down. The cook sat up and choked.

"What did you do that for?" Curly asked. He looked around

157

and wondered what he was doing in the kitchen. The last thing that he could remember was cornering the Fleet kid in the caretaker's cottage. Suddenly the fog cleared. "Don't eat anything! It's all laced with salt tablets!"

Bucky spit out a mouthful of chili and shoved the bowl aside. The nurse followed suit. Big Al aimed his blaster at them. "Uh-uh. Keep eating."

Nurse Knockwurst and Bucky exchanged an uneasy glance. The ax had just fallen.

"Make a plate for yourself and join them," Big Al said to Curly.

"The chili is laced with salt tablets," Curly repeated as he filled his plate.

"I know," Big Al said. He kept the blaster pointed at them until they finished every drop. Big Al tossed them the carton of spiked Twinkies. "Who wants dessert?"

"I think you're being unfair," Nurse Knockwurst grumbled.

"I agree," Bucky added. "It was Curly's fault, not ours."

"Take it up with the kidnappers union," Big Al replied, motioning with his blaster for them to eat. A few seconds after they finished the last Twinkie in the box, the salt tablets kicked in. Big Al watched his crew members grimace in pain as their transformation began. For a brief moment their alien bodies appeared and then their DNA combined with their costumes, locking them into their human forms. "Once the mission is complete, Nurse Knockwurst will distribute the antidote and you'll get your share of the loot. One more screwup and I'll leave you to rot in those bodies. Do we understand one another?"

His crew shook their human heads as Big Al got up from the table and stormed out of the kitchen, slamming the door behind him. Nurse Knockwurst and Bucky glared at the cook.

"Okay, so it wasn't one of my best meals," Curly said sheepishly.

CHAPTER

Day Seven — 9:45 P.M.

I'm worried about Greeley," Einstein said as he paced back and forth across the cottage. It was his turn to stand watch while Roxie tried to get some sleep. They had agreed to alternate every three hours. Einstein stopped at the window and scanned the area around the barn for any sign of activity. Satisfied that they were safe, he moved away from the window and resumed pacing.

"Greeley knows what he's up against," Roxie replied softly. "He's been through this before."

"What are you talking about?"

"Over forty years ago Greeley was faced with the same situation. Big Al won that round. The kids were abducted and Sleepy Time was destroyed. Two years later Big Al came back and killed him to make sure that there were no loose ends."

"I wondered why Greeley was involved in this."

"Well, now you know," Roxie said, her voice tense. "Greeley has a score to settle."

Suddenly, Einstein had an idea. "If Greeley can get inside the ship, we may have a chance," he told Roxie. "All he has to do is stick to Big Al like glue until he receives the coordinates. Once we have the location, IMPS can handle the rest."

"Mucho Fahn is far too clever to be fooled that easily," Roxie said, shaking her head. "If he doesn't hear from Big Al exactly five minutes before the wormhole opens, Mucho Fahn will automatically move the zoo to another location. I intend to sneak aboard the ship and hitch a ride through the wormhole, the same way that I got here. IMPS isn't going to help, Fleet. I'm flying solo on this one."

"What are you talking about?" Einstein asked.

Tears welled up in the corners of her eyes and dribbled down her cheeks. "IMPS dropped the investigation over two years ago. Mucho Fahn bought them off. This is Big Al's last mission. If it's aborted, I may never find Mucho's monster zoo. That's a risk I'm not willing to take. Greeley isn't the only one with a score to settle with these gangsters."

"What do you mean?" Einstein asked.

"They kidnapped my little brother!" Roxie cried. "Three years ago they came to my planet and took him. He's out there somewhere, Fleet. I can feel it."

Einstein lay down beside Roxie and held her gently in his arms. "I'm sorry. What can I do to help?"

"I want you to get out of here in one piece," Roxie sobbed. "I've already lost one person I love. Losing another would be too much to bear."

Einstein held her closer and squeezed her tight. The moment was suddenly broken by a rustling sound coming from outside the cottage. Einstein sat up and it stopped. "Did you hear that?" he whispered to Roxie.

161

She sat up and drew her blaster. Roxie put her finger to her lips and motioned for Einstein to be still. There was definitely someone or something outside the cottage, moving slowly toward the window. It was tapping softly against the pane of glass. The first tap was at the top. The next one was on the bottom. The frequency increased as the tapping grew louder. The drumroll echoed throughout the cottage and then stopped. The silence was deafening, but not as deafening as the roar that followed. Suddenly, the window shattered into pieces, sending shards of glass flying through the cottage. One by one, ten black Tootsie Pop eyes poked through the window and peeked into the cottage, all of them staring at Einstein.

"Move back, Fleet!" Roxie warned him, but it was already too late. The gloka had him by the ankle and was dragging him across the floor. Roxie aimed at the scaly red tentacle and fired twice. The gloka released its grip and retreated.

Einstein jumped up and ran to Roxie. They moved to the farthest point away from the window and waited for the gloka to make its next move. "I thought we killed all the glokas," Einstein said, his voice trembling with fear.

"Must have missed one," Roxie whispered. "I guess the campfire stories about Godzilla were true." The female roared again, rattling the walls. Suddenly, she burst through the side of the cottage. Before Roxie could fire a shot, the gloka was on top of her. "Run, Fleet!" she screamed.

Einstein ignored her and picked up a piece of wood. He clubbed the gloka over the head as hard as he could, hoping it would release Roxie. He swung again, but the female was too fast. Godzilla's powerful jaws turned the two-by-four into a toothpick, leaving Einstein defenseless. The female tossed Roxie across the cottage and turned her complete and undivided attention to Einstein. Roxie's head hit the wall hard and she didn't get up. Einstein couldn't tell if she was alive or dead, but there was no way to get to her. Godzilla slowly moved forward. Einstein closed his eyes, hoping that the end would be quick and merciful. A barrage of blue beams suddenly filled the cottage, striking the female all over her body. Einstein could smell her burning flesh.

As Godzilla backed away, he could hear Big Al shouting, "Keep firing, you idiots!" Bucky and Nurse Knockwurst were both crouched military style with their blasters blazing, while Curly stood there and threw dirt clods. Godzilla roared at them and cautiously backed away. The blasts bounced off her thick metallic scales. It was like throwing rocks at a tank. While she was distracted, Einstein took advantage of opportunity. He turned tail and ran, quickly putting some distance between himself and the cottage. Curly watched as Einstein disappeared into the desert night. The female seemed to have lost her taste for the blaster battle and retreated in the same direction.

"I thought you said she was dead," Big Al said, glaring at Curly. "Can't you do anything right?"

Bucky nudged Big Al and pointed at the rubble. "It's the girl," he said.

"Is that the IMPS agent?" he asked Curly. The cook nodded, afraid to speak. Big Al picked up the blaster and tossed it to him. "I believe this is yours."

"She's still alive," Nurse Knockwurst said. "Do you want me to finish her?"

163

Big Al shook his head. "Take her to the spaceship. We'll lock down and spend the night there in case the female decides to return. I'm not taking any more chances."

"What about Fleet?" Bucky asked.

"If the female doesn't get him, the desert will," Big Al replied. "Either way, he's dead."

CHAPTER 35

Day Eight — 10:53 A.M.

"We deserve to be locked up," Shirley moaned.

"What are you talking about?" Norman wondered if his wife had cracked under the pressure after spending the night in jail. He had read about such things but had little practical experience in the matter, being a first-time offender.

"We're bad parents," Shirley said, looking him dead in the eye. "Who sends their son to camp for the summer without investigating it first? Now he's missing. Einstein is going to end up as one of those kids with his picture on the side of a milk carton, and it's all our fault."

"Don't be ridiculous," he replied. Norman had never seen his wife act so irrational. She paced across the eight-by-ten cell like a caged animal, inspecting every nook and cranny. Suddenly, she stopped at the window and clawed at the stucco beneath the bars. "What are you doing?" Norman asked.

"I'm busting us out," Shirley whispered. "Don't just stand there, help me."

"Are you crazy?" he said. "That redneck sheriff will put us away for life if he catches you."

"Either you're with me or you're against me, Norman," Shirley said, tugging at the steel bars. "It's time to choose sides."

"What are you talking about? We've been married for twenty years."

"Prison changes people."

The Fleets were so preoccupied that they failed to notice Chief Chester standing in front of the cell, observing the domestic dispute with amusement. A large man stood beside him, trying not to laugh.

"Enjoying your stay in Saugus, folks?" the chief asked pleasantly, dangling a large silver ring of keys like a prize.

Shirley rushed at the chief. She reached through the bars, desperately trying to rip the key ring from his grasp. The chief was surprisingly agile for a big man and easily eluded her. "You can't keep us locked up in this cell like animals!" Shirley screamed.

"Don't intend to, Mrs. Fleet," the chief said calmly as he opened the door to the cell. "You're both free to go."

Norman and Shirley eyed the chief with suspicion.

"Who is that?" Norman asked, pointing at the large man next to Chief Chester.

"This is Mr. Armstrong. His son, Billy, is also missing. He got the same brochure in the mail that you folks did and came here to check on his son."

"Just call me Joe," the big man said, extending a hairy, calloused hand that smelled like fish. "I haven't spoken with my boy since he left, so I decided to drive up to Camp Creepy Time to make sure that he hadn't killed someone. Figured I'd check in with the police department first. Billy's spent more time in jail than he has in school. The kid's a menace, but he's all I got. His mom ran off with a traveling salesman a few days after he was born and left him behind. She must have been psychic."

Mr. Armstrong looked as if he had just rolled out of bed. His clothes were a mess and his hair hadn't been combed in days. Despite the fact that he was tall and lanky, his belly ballooned over the top of his black leather belt. As far as personal hygiene went, the man had none. He smelled like he'd been wrestling in pig slop.

"We think the kids have been kidnapped," Norman said, walking out of the cell.

"That's not all," Shirley added. "Our son said that the nurse was conducting medical experiments on the campers and turning them into mindless zombies."

"You don't say," Joe replied, clearly interested.

"Are you a scientist?" Norman asked.

"I'm a freelance photographer. I snap paparazzi shots to pay the bills, but the big bucks are in the weird stuff."

"Tell him about the ghost," Shirley said to her husband.

"The camp is haunted?" Joe said, rubbing his hands together. "What are we waiting for? Let's go check it out."

Chief Chester shook his head and sighed. "That's the problem, I'm afraid. You folks were right. I checked it out and the camp doesn't exist. Your kids could be anywhere."

"What about Sleepy Time?" Norman said. "The old guy at the filling station said there used to be a camp out here by that name. Why don't we drive out there and check it out?"

167

"That camp was shut down before I was even born."

"Call Warner and ask him for directions," Norman demanded.

"I don't know if he's going to be of much help," Chief Chester replied. "He's still pretty pissed about you running off without paying for your gas."

"This should cover the gas," Norman said, handing the chief a twenty-dollar bill. "Tell Warner that I'll give him another twenty for directions."

"You don't get out much, do you?" Chief Chester replied. "You owe him over a hundred dollars."

"For a tank of gasoline?" Norman asked. "That's highway robbery."

"Take it up with OPEC," the policeman suggested.

"I hope Warner takes credit cards." Norman sighed. He looked at his wife and shook his head. "Remind me to trade the Volvo wagon in for a hybrid when this is over."

CHAPTER 36

Day Eight — 12:06 P.M.

The sun beat down on the back of Einstein's neck like a red-hot branding iron. He was tired and thirsty and his muscles were cramped. Worst of all, he was lost. In retrospect, he should have paid more attention to the survival techniques that he had been forced to endure as a Cub Scout, but who knew that it would one day be a matter of life or death? In truth it didn't matter. Whether the sun rose in the west or set in the east, Einstein had no clue where he was going. The nearest town was at least twenty or thirty miles from the camp as the crow flies. Unfortunately, he wasn't a crow. He was a boy who was hopelessly lost in the desert and suffering from heatstroke. Suddenly he realized that his odds of survival were slim at best. He sat down in the sand, unzipped his pack, and removed a couple of Twinkies.

"Might as well die a happy camper," Einstein mused as he positioned the Twinkies in a neat row on the top of his backpack. As he selected his first victim, his mind began to wander. He had always assumed that his life would flash before his eyes just moments before the end, but he never expected the end to come so soon. At the tender age of thirteen, there was only so much one could reflect upon. Einstein had to admit that the last week at Creepy Time had been an adventure. Too bad he wouldn't live to tell the tale, but who would have believed him anyhow?

He unwrapped his next victim and examined it closely. He had eaten countless thousands of Twinkies in his lifetime, but this one was special. This was going to be the last. "Here's looking at you, kid." Einstein took a big bite and chewed slowly, savoring the experience. A feeling of tranquility spread through his being and he felt at peace with the world. The desert began to fade away and Einstein found himself floating inside a thick, silver cloud of spun silk. Instead of being soft and billowy, the cloud was sticky and gooey, like the cream-filled center of a giant Twinkie.

Einstein recalled a documentary that he had seen on the Discovery Channel in which a Native American shaman ingested magic herbs to induce visions of the afterlife. The tribe was from the very same area in which he now stood. It only made sense that, in his vision quest, Einstein would become one with the Twinkie. With some difficulty, he took another bite out of the magic pastry, hoping to learn more about the unknown mysteries of this life before going to the next world.

"I'm listening," he said softly, cupping the remains of the Twinkie in his outstretched palm. "Tell me, what is the secret of life?"

"How should I know?" a muffled voice replied.

Einstein was expecting to hear something more enlightening, but what could one expect from a pastry? He took another bite, hoping that the magic Twinkie would elaborate on the message, but it refused to say more. All he could hear was the eerie silence of the Mojave Desert. The cloud of silver engulfed his body as the sun slowly disappeared and was eclipsed by a dark shadow. Obviously the Twinkie would not reveal the secret to life in this world. Perhaps it would be revealed in the next. He had begun to drift off when he felt the hand of God reach down and grab him by the collar. Einstein couldn't believe his luck. He hadn't been in heaven ten seconds and he was already going to get an audience with the Almighty. "So, there is a heaven." He sighed.

He waited for God to speak and reveal the secret of life. "WAKE UP, YOU IDIOT!" Granted, it wasn't exactly the divine message that Einstein had expected to hear, but he supposed that he deserved it for living the life of a slacker. He heard the Almighty roaring at him. Einstein thought he would be forgiven in the end, not yelled at for a laundry list of past offenses. Suddenly, a thought occurred to Einstein. If he were in heaven, then why was it so dark? Was it possible that he had miscalculated his situation altogether? Would he have to serve eternal detention in the fiery pits of hell?

"I REPENT!" Einstein listed everything that he could think of that he had ever done wrong and even confessed to a few things he hadn't done, figuring it would score some brownie points with the man upstairs. Suddenly, he was jerked out of the darkness and back into the world. "THANK YOU, GOD! YOU WON'T REGRET IT!"

The next thing he knew, Einstein was sitting in the passenger seat of Greeley's old truck. The old ghost was sitting next to him, driving like a madman. Einstein rubbed his temples and tried to clear away the cobwebs. He wasn't in heaven or hell, he was back in the desert, which left another possibility. Like Greeley, he would spend the rest of eternity at Creepy Time. He shuddered at the thought. "Am I dead?" Einstein asked the ghost.

"Not yet, but the day is still young," Greeley cackled.

"What happened?" Einstein asked, rubbing his head.

"I followed the sound of incoherent babbling and it led me right to you."

"I was drifting among silver clouds," Einstein said, still in a daze. "It was beautiful."

"Those silver clouds were made out of spun metal. They were cocoons. You were resting your weary head on the missing campers," Greeley informed him. "Godzilla was about to add you to her collection when I came along. I ran her off with my truck and pulled you out of there. You owe me big-time, Houdini."

"What happened to Godzilla?" Einstein asked.

"Look behind you," Greeley said, looking in his rear-view mirror.

Einstein turned around and felt a chill run down his spine. Godzilla was right behind them and closing ground quickly.

"I told you the day was still young." Greeley sighed.

Einstein got his first good look at the female. Godzilla was bigger than a bull elephant and, like the elephant, she was surprisingly fast for a creature so large. She used all eight of her muscular legs in perfect unison and easily maneuvered the rough desert terrain. Her coat was bloodred and protected with armor-plated scales. Two razor-sharp silver fangs protruded from the top of her mouth. She was drooling in anticipation of the kill, which was less than ten yards away. "Can't this old heap go any faster, Greeley?"

"Nope."

Einstein was hoping to hear something more encouraging, even if it was a lie. If they couldn't outrun the creature, they were goners. While he was in a rational state of panic, Greeley seemed irrationally calm. In fact, he actually seemed to be enjoying himself. "What are you grinning about, you old ghost?" Einstein asked.

"I got me a plan."

Einstein was hoping for more information, but there wasn't time. Godzilla caught up to the truck and jumped onto the back end of the flatbed. Her weight lifted the front end off the ground, causing the truck to pop a wheelie.

"Yahoo!" Greeley hollered. "Tell me this ain't a pisser!"

"This is suicide," Einstein mumbled to himself.

As Greeley maneuvered on two wheels, Godzilla tenaciously clung to the edge of the flatbed and refused to let go. Slowly but surely, she managed to crawl toward the cab. Once she reached the middle of the flatbed, the redistribution of weight brought the front end of the pickup back to Earth and the momentum tossed Godzilla right into the back of the cab. All that now separated her from her prey was the back window. She rammed her head against the glass and it exploded, shattering into hundreds of little pieces. Godzilla locked her muscular appendages around the cab and roared at them through the glassless opening.

Einstein was paralyzed with fear. He could literally feel

Godzilla breathing down the back of his neck, her powerful jaws gaping and preparing to tear him to pieces. He opened his pocketknife and stabbed the creature, trying to penetrate her thick coat of armor. The tempered steel blade snapped off at the hilt. Einstein sank down into the seat and looked up. All he could see was a dark hole filled with rows of sharp metallic fangs. It was like staring into the gaping mouth of a giant great white shark. She lunged at Einstein repeatedly, but her head was too large to fit through the opening. He picked up his backpack and used it like a shield. Godzilla sank her fangs into the pack and tried to pull Einstein out the back window. He braced his legs, using the floorboard of the truck as leverage, and wedged the pack in her jaws. "I could use some help here, Greeley!"

"Let go of the pack!" Greeley shouted.

"No way!" Einstein shouted back.

Just as Einstein was about to be pulled out the back window, Greeley reached over and tickled him. "Coochie. Coochie."

Einstein grabbed at the ghost's bony fingers and let go of his backpack. As he did, Godzilla rolled backward. She tossed aside Einstein's backpack and quickly crawled back to the cab. Unable to get through the opening, she changed her plan of attack. Godzilla climbed on top of the cab and sank two large fangs straight through the roof, missing Greeley and Einstein by inches. She tried to pull her fangs out, but couldn't. They were stuck.

"Hang on, Houdini!" Greeley shouted, pointing a bony finger at the barn. "We're almost there! Get ready to jump!"

"Are you crazy?" Einstein shouted at the ghost.

"You have a better idea?" Greeley asked. The barn was about fifty yards ahead and there was no time to argue. The ghost opened his door and disappeared, leaving no one to drive. The truck was on a collision course with the barn and there was no way to stop it.

"No guts, no glory," Einstein told himself as he opened the door and jumped. He fell on his side hard and rolled for about ten yards, barely missing a cactus. Seconds later the pickup truck slammed into the side of the barn and exploded into flames. Einstein got up slowly and watched it burn. As he did, Greeley appeared beside him, holding his backpack. "I think this belongs to you."

"Thanks," Einstein said as he slung the pack over his shoulder. He looked at the barn and sighed. "I'm going to miss you, pal."

"What are you talking about, Houdini?"

"I'm going to go and get on the ship," Einstein said as he began to walk away. "Without the antidote, I might as well go with them."

"The antidote is on the ship." Greeley smiled at him.

Einstein stopped dead in his tracks. "What did you say?"

"You heard me, Houdini. I say it's time for a little payback," the ghost said. "Are you with me, boy?"

Einstein smiled at the ghost. "Let's go finish this thing."

CHAPTER

Day Eight — 1:02 P.M.

Nurse Knockwurst's lab was located on the third floor of the spaceship. It was a sterile environment, equipped with an examination table and lots of high-tech medical equipment. After her capture, they had taken Roxie to the lab. She was hanging upside down from a thick metal rod, her hands and feet bound with plastic tubing, like a piñata at a Mexican fiesta. Nurse Knockwurst pushed Roxie gently, swinging her back and forth. Every so often, she would give her a stiff shove, sending Roxie crashing headfirst into the wall. Her IMPS training had taught Roxie to endure endless hours of pain during interrogation. More important, her training had taught her patience. Sooner or later, the bad guys would let their guard down and she would make her move. Roxie hoped it would be sooner. She had a splitting headache.

"I'm impressed," Big Al told Roxie. "You are the first one to ever penetrate our operation. How did you do it?"

"It was easy. I just followed the trail of slime."

Big Al laughed at her joke. He actually admired the IMPS agent's bravado. For one so young, she had guts and spunk. If there were more time, he would have enjoyed sticking around and watching her squirm, but time was growing short. The wormhole would open in less than two hours and he had to confirm the coordinates. With so much at stake, Big Al made the prudent decision to put business before pleasure. "I'm going to contact Mucho Fahn," he whispered to Nurse Knockwurst. "After you break our brave little friend and find Fleet, you can eliminate her. I don't want any loose ends."

The nurse took Big Al's hand and caressed it softly. "Hurry back, you big galoot," she cooed. "I have special plans for the two of us tonight."

Big Al smiled. "We'll relax as soon as the ship takes off and not a moment sooner. After that, it's time to uncork the champagne." Big Al blew her a kiss and walked away.

Nurse Knockwurst watched him leave with stars in her eyes and then turned her attention back to Roxie. "Now, where were we?"

"Big Al is your boyfriend?" Roxie giggled. "I hope you two aren't planning on having kids."

Nurse Knockwurst was not amused. She reached inside a cupboard and carefully removed a large glass jar. It was crawling with several big black scorpions. Nurse Knockwurst held the jar up to Roxie's face and shook it, agitating the creatures inside. "Did you know that scorpions are carnivores? They paralyze their prey with the stingers on their tails. The pain is excruciating. As a rule, most scorpions can't inject enough venom to kill something your size. Bark scorpions are an exception to that rule and you're looking at six of them. They are quite lethal, I'm afraid."

"Go ahead and do it," Roxie said defiantly.

"Poor creatures haven't had a bite in days," the nurse cooed as she slowly unscrewed the lid. The angry scorpions were already climbing toward the top of the jar, eager to get to work. "Come and get it, boys."

"Welcome to Camp Creepy Time," Einstein said, standing in the doorway. "If the food doesn't kill you, the counselors will."

"We've been looking for you," Nurse Knockwurst growled.

"At your service," Einstein replied gallantly. He stood on one foot and curled his fingers into claws, mimicking an awkward fighting stance that he'd seen in an old kung fu movie. He motioned at Nurse Knockwurst with his fingers to make the first move.

"You want a piece of me?" Knockwurst growled. "Come to momma."

He was half as tall as the nurse and she outweighed him by at least one hundred pounds, but Einstein stood his ground.

"Be careful, Fleet," Roxie shouted. "She's a trained killer."

"Don't worry about me, babe," Einstein said with confidence. "I can handle this hag with one hand tied behind my back." To illustrate the point, Einstein put one hand behind his back and made an indecent gesture at the nurse with the other.

Nurse Knockwurst flew into a rage and charged at him like a bull, screaming at the top of her lungs. She lifted the scorpion jar over her head and prepared to hurl it at Einstein. "You're going to regret that, chubby!"

Much to Roxie's surprise, Einstein stood his ground. Suddenly, his other hand appeared from behind his back, holding his homemade peashooter. "Say hello to my little friend."

Nurse Knockwurst looked at him and laughed. "Are you kidding me?"

Einstein smiled at her as he loaded a marble into the makeshift weapon. "You messed with the wrong camper," he said as he aimed the peashooter at the nurse. Einstein took a deep breath and blew hard, raising his aim at just the last second. It was a direct hit. The glass shattered on impact, freeing the deadly scorpions inside. Two of them landed on her oversized bun and were cautiously climbing down. They reminded Einstein of rock climbers, rappelling down a vertical cliff. Three others clung to Nurse Knockwurst's white dress, stinging her repeatedly through the thin cotton material. The last scorpion landed on one of her shoes. It climbed up to her ankle and began to attack.

In a matter of seconds, the venom began to take its toll. Nurse Knockwurst felt woozy and her vision blurred. She saw two of everything, including Einstein. She lunged at the wrong one and missed, running headfirst into a metal filing cabinet. Nurse Knockwurst moaned and then collapsed on the floor, curled up in a ball. Einstein knelt down, put two fingers to her neck, and felt her pulse to make sure that she wasn't playing possum.

"Is she dead?" Roxie asked.

"She's fine, but I can't say the same for the scorpions," he replied, pointing at the floor. All six scorpions were also curled up in fetal positions. Einstein kicked one of them across the room to be sure. It ricocheted off the wall and lay there. He picked up another, examined it, and then tossed it aside.

"I thought you were afraid of spiders," Roxie said.

"These little things?" Einstein snickered. He walked up to Roxie and gave her a twirl. "Want to hang out for a while?"

"Get me down, Fleet," she said. "We've got work to do."

Einstein cut her down and untied her. They wasted no time securing the nurse. She was already showing signs of life, despite the massive dose of venom flowing through her system. With some difficulty, Roxie and Einstein hoisted her off the floor and laid her on the examination table. They secured her body to the table with electrician's tape, making sure that she couldn't move a muscle. Einstein had learned a trick or two from his stay in the infirmary.

Roxie pulled Einstein aside and spoke to him. Capturing Nurse Knockwurst was one thing, but squeezing the location of the antidote out of her was an entirely different matter. The woman was a hardened criminal and wouldn't break easily. Most people were squeamish when it came to this sort of thing. She wondered if Einstein was one of them. "Are you sure that you can handle this?"

"I'm in seventh grade. Trust me, I know a little something about torture. Give me fifteen minutes with the old crone and she'll be singing like a canary." He filled a pail with water and dumped it over the nurse's head. "Wakey, wakey."

Nurse Knockwurst woke up groggy and mean. She struggled to free herself, but to no avail. Unable to do anything else, she gave Einstein the evil eye. "When I get loose, I'm going to turn you into an oversized pretzel," she threatened.

Einstein ignored her. It wasn't the first time that someone had threatened to do him bodily harm. "Where is the antidote? We can do this the easy way or the hard way. The choice is up to you."

"I'm not going to tell you a thing, you little twerp."

"We"ll see about that." He walked around the table and considered how to best approach the situation. The nurse was already bound to the table with sixteen rolls of electrician's tape. Normally, the next step would be to lock her in the janitor's closet until recess. Unfortunately, there wasn't one in the lab and the nurse was too large to stuff into a cabinet. Einstein decided to go with a couple of the old tried-and-true methods, starting with lugie torture. He climbed up on the table and leaned over her, positioning his mouth directly in line with her mouth and began to drool. He let the strand get within an inch of her lips and then sucked it back in. Einstein repeated the process a few times, but the results were minimal at best.

"That the best you got, chubby?" the nurse challenged.

"I was just getting warmed up." Einstein could see that the old bird was going to be a tough nut to crack. He would have to up the price of poker. There was torture and then there was torture, but one was feared above all others. It was time to pull out the big guns. He covered her head with a bedsheet and climbed under with her.

"You going to read me a bedtime story?" the nurse asked.

Einstein ignored her and concentrated on the job at hand. He mustered up thoughts of the chili con carne that they served in school and let loose with his first shot. It was an

SBD, the most deadly fart in his arsenal. Although one couldn't hear a disgusting flatulent sound with the "silent but deadly" brand, it was normally twice as smelly as the run-of-the-mill fart. This one was no exception. The nurse began to gag and then went ballistic.

"You call that a fart, you little pig! Try this on for size." Nurse Knockwurst fired off a shot of her own, and it was an A-bomb. Obviously, the woman was no stranger to this game. Einstein threw off the sheet and ran for cover. Nurse Knock-wurst laughed at him. "There's plenty more where that came from, porky!"

Einstein walked away from the table and stood next to Roxie. Both of them were holding their noses. "She's one tough old bird," Einstein whispered.

"Let me give it a try," Roxie said, setting the blaster to sting and blowing a hole through the middle of her bun. The smell of singed hair filled the lab. Nurse Knockwurst watched as Roxie adjusted the setting on the blaster from sting to kill. "Where is the antidote?"

"It's in that cabinet over there," the nurse screamed. "The key is on the chain around my neck."

"Why didn't I think of that?" Einstein said, smiling at Roxie. He yanked the chain from the nurse's neck and went to see if she was telling the truth. On the top shelf was a large jar filled with square black pills, just where Nurse Knockwurst said they would be.

"I see she blabbed," Greeley said, materializing by the table.

"They always do, comrade," Einstein replied.

Nurse Knockwurst stared at the ghost in disbelief. "We killed you," she said. Her jaw dropped and Einstein took the opportunity to gag her. He'd heard enough from the good nurse for one day.

CHAPTER 38

Day Eight — 1:35 P.M.

Greeley guided Einstein and Roxie to the containment area, which was located on the second level of the ship. The campers were sound asleep, safely packed in individual pods. Four sets of steel manacles secured their hands and feet. As an extra precaution, electrician's tape had been liberally wrapped around their bodies, anchoring them to their beds. A clear dome covered each pod, making it possible to look inside. "Anyone care for monster under glass?" Einstein joked. "It's the special today."

Roxie walked up to one of the pods and pulled the latch underneath. The clear dome immediately sprang open and a familiar stench filled the room. "It's Billy Armstrong," she said. "He's not asleep—he's been sedated."

"Why don't we leave him there?" Einstein said. Roxie glared at him. "It was just a suggestion."

"It was your idea to free the campers, remember?" she reminded him. "So, let's get to work. I figure that we have less than an hour to distribute the antidote, somehow get them untied, and sneak them off the ship. That doesn't leave us a lot of time."

"How do you know the antidote works?" Greeley asked. "Nurse Knockwurst could have lied."

"He's right," Einstein said. He opened the jar and removed four black tablets. The label said to take one to two pills a day over a few days. The campers would return to normal in less than a week. They had less than an hour.

"What are you doing, Fleet?" Roxie asked.

"Greeley's right," he said, swallowing the tablets. "We need a guinea pig."

A minute or two passed and nothing happened, so Einstein doubled the dosage. Roxie tried to stop him, but he knew that there was no other way. A couple more minutes passed, but nothing happened. His body was still covered with patches of brown fur. Nonetheless, Einstein felt different. Suddenly, his crotch began to itch.

"It's not working." Roxie sighed.

Einstein turned around and looked down the front of his pants. "It's working," he said, his voice cracking. "Give everyone eight tablets of the antidote and remember to save some for the eleven missing campers."

Roxie shook her head. "We know that the antidote works, but we still can't be sure that a massive dose won't have adverse effects. Let's start with two tablets each, just to be on the safe side." She poured most of the tablets into the inside pocket of Einstein's pack. It was a subtle reminder to Einstein that she would not be coming with him. He would be responsible for administering the rest of the antidote, if they made it to safety.

Roxie and Einstein started opening the pods, releasing the

manacles, and administering the antidote to the campers, while Greeley stood guard by the door. The ghost had seen Big Al in the main cabin of the ship, waiting for Mucho Fahn to send down the coordinates. Bucky and Curly, however, were nowhere to be found. Roxie assumed that they were in the engine room, checking to make sure that all of the equipment was in working order.

"Whoever tied these guys up knew what they were doing," Roxie said, examining one of the campers. She pulled a mean-looking switchblade from her pants pocket and flipped open the blade. "Do you still have your pocketknife?" she asked Einstein.

He shook his head. "It's a long story," he said, smiling at Greeley. "If we live through this, remind me to tell you about it one day."

Roxie looked at Greeley and had an idea. "Do you think that you could transport all of the campers outside the ship?" she asked the ghost.

"I could take two or three," he said, "but not all of them. Even if I could, we would still need to cut them loose. We'd have to be connected in a circle."

"We need another knife or a pair of sharp scissors," Roxie said. "We'll never make it in time otherwise."

"I'll go look," Einstein volunteered.

As he started for the door, Roxie called to him. He turned and she tossed him her blaster. "Be careful, comrade."

CHAPTER 39

Day Eight — 2:00 P.M.

Einstein jogged down to the main cabin of the ship and quietly looked around. He saw a sharp object that looked like a pair of scissors sitting on one of the consoles, but they were impossible to get at without being seen. Big Al was sitting in the middle of the room, leaning back in his swivel chair with both feet resting on the control panel. He seemed preoccupied. Every few seconds, he would look at his watch and stare at the control panel. Einstein used the opportunity to sneak into the control room and hide beneath one of the empty stations.

"Who's there?" Big Al said, noticing a movement out of the corner of his eye. He drew his blaster and looked around the room. Big Al looked at his watch again.

In less than thirty seconds Mucho Fahn would make contact. Once Big Al confirmed that the mission was complete and it was safe, Mucho Fahn would provide him with the coordinates. That would leave exactly thirty minutes before the force field surrounded the barn. The plasma shield was designed to contain the damage to the immediate area around the barn during liftoff. There was no sense destroying Earth in the process of a routine kidnapping. Once the force field was engaged, the wormhole would open and the ship would be transported millions of miles through space in a matter of seconds. Big Al smiled. In a few more days he'd be kicking back on the blue beaches of the planet Pomdor. While he sipped Flaming Purple Peacocks at his leisure, his money would be earning a cool eight percent. Whoever said that crime didn't pay wasn't very good at it.

The red button on the control panel lit up, indicating that the transmission had begun. Big Al put on the headset and listened to the voice on the other end.

"Do you have my monsters?" Mucho Fahn asked. He was direct and to the point, as always.

"All of them," Big Al replied, "and some new material for you to review."

"More Earth stories?" Mucho replied. "How interesting."

The "Earth stories" Mucho was referring to were movies. Big Al had brought old black-and-white monster classics back to Mucho Fahn the last time he was on the planet. He knew that they would fascinate Mucho even if he didn't fully comprehend that they were only make-believe.

Mucho Fahn had been watching the same movies for over forty years. With the passing of each year, his desire to add the monsters from the "Earth stories" to his zoo had increased until it became an obsession. He was willing to pay a prince's ransom for each and every werewolf, mummy, and vampire that Big Al could capture. The problem was that they didn't exist other than on film.

That all changed when Big Al heard about Nurse Knockwurst's discovery of the salt tablets. They had quickly formed a partnership, put together a new crew, and headed back to his old stomping grounds in the middle of the Mojave Desert. Now that the salt tablets had transformed the campers into monsters just as the nurse had promised, it was payday.

"Bring them to me," Mucho demanded. "Your money is waiting, along with a substantial bonus if these Earth stories are as good as the last."

Big Al had anticipated this response from Mucho. In fact, he had counted on it. He knew that once Mucho had his monsters, Big Al didn't stand a chance of getting paid, let alone staying alive, unless he had more to offer in the future. Mucho would get rid of all of them. "Just wait until you see the monsters in these modern stories. Looks like I'm going to have to put off retirement for a while," Big Al lied. "There's a fortune to be made on this planet."

The transmission went dead.

Big Al looked down at the panel and saw the coordinates begin to appear. He stood up and stretched. It would take a few minutes to finish, and watching it wouldn't make it happen any faster. Suddenly, he sensed another movement. This time he was certain. He looked over at the navigation station and saw a hand reaching for a pair of scissors that someone had carelessly left on the console. The chubby paw looked very familiar. "What are you doing, Fleet?"

"I was looking for the arts and crafts center," Einstein said, coming out of hiding. "I was going to make you a lanyard as a going-away present."

"Still the camp clown, I see." He picked Einstein up with one hand and tossed him across the room. "I should have done that the first time I laid eyes on you."

Einstein got up and pointed the business end of the blaster at Big Al's chest.

Big Al smiled. "I underestimated you, Fleet, but it won't happen again."

"Let's make it interesting, shall we?" Einstein said softly. He placed the blaster in his belt and walked toward Big Al. The two of them circled each other, jockeying for position.

"I'm an expert with this weapon, son." Big Al laughed. "You have guts; I'll give you that. You have any smart-ass remarks to make before I spill your guts all over my nice clean floor?"

"Yeah. This camp sucks!" Einstein said. "Now quit stalling and make your move. I haven't got all day."

"So long, chubby!"

Big Al drew, but Einstein was faster. The boy fired a single shot and hit Big Al dead center in the chest. A blue field from the surge of the blaster surrounded him as he dropped to his knees. He stared at Einstein in disbelief. "Where did you learn to shoot like that?"

"Video games," Einstein replied.

Big Al leaned over and pushed one of the buttons on the control panel. "The clock is ticking."

Einstein looked down at the rectangular window on the panel. A series of black numbers flashed across a white screen. It was a very long sequence and it was constantly changing. Einstein suspected that the transporter was calculating the coordinates to lock in location, taking into account all of the variables such as planet rotation, gravitational pull, and other factors. Suddenly it stopped. As soon as it did, the panel next to it lit up and another series of numbers appeared. Big Al was right. Thirty minutes counting down. Einstein removed his journal from his backpack and jotted down a note. He put it back and headed for the door.

"This isn't over, Fleet," Big Al said as he collapsed on the floor.

Einstein watched as Big Al began to melt. It was like watching a fire in a wax museum. "It is for you, pal," Einstein said.

CHAPTER

40

Day Eight — 2:08 P.M.

Einstein ran back up to the holding area as fast as he could. As he passed through the door, it seemed as if little progress had been made since he left. About half of the campers had been stripped of tape and none of them was awake. He was even more surprised to see Roxie and Greeley standing there doing nothing. "There's no time for a coffee break, guys. Everyone get back to work!"

Einstein felt something cold and hard pressed against his back. "Put your hands up," Bucky ordered as he reached into Einstein's belt and took away the blaster. "Where's Big Al?"

"He's up in the main cabin," Einstein replied. "When I left, he was having a meltdown. The man's been under a great deal of stress lately."

"And Nurse Knockwurst?"

"She's in the lab, catching up on her beauty sleep."

"I can't take any more of this, kid," Curly said. He pointed his blaster at Einstein and waved good-bye. "So long, camper."

Bucky grabbed his arm and stopped him. "Not yet," he said. "We still need to find the antidote. Where is it, Fleet?"

"I don't know what you're talking about," Einstein lied.

Bucky looked at the cook. "Check out his . . . Mmmmm!"

"What's a Mmmmm?" Curly asked.

The alien's face was ashen. "Look behind you, man."

The cook turned around and found himself face-to-face with one of the mummies. Manny picked Curly up and squeezed him until he dropped his weapon. "Let go of me, you bag of rags!" the cook screamed, gasping for breath. The mummy obeyed and dropped him on his head. Curly hit the floor and tried to reach for his blaster. Manny pinned the cook's gun hand beneath his foot.

Einstein knelt down and picked up the weapon. "Thanks, Manny," he said to the mummy. "I owe you one."

The mummy gave Einstein a big bandaged thumbs-up, and then stomped on the cook's back for good measure. "Mmmmm!"

Bucky was surrounded by a couple of vampires and were-wolves. One of the werewolves had taken his blaster and had him covered. The vampires were eyeing him like a hot meal. "Is there time for a little snack?" Vinnie asked, staring at Bucky's neck.

Einstein shook his head. "Maybe later," he replied. Einstein surveyed the room. All of the campers were awake, but only half had been untied. He looked at his watch. Only twenty minutes left to free the rest and get them clear of the barn. "Right now we have work to do."

The antidote had partially worked. The campers still looked like monsters, but they seemed cognizant of their human side. Einstein put the monster half to work. He ordered the camp-ers who were free to help free the others. The werewolves and vampires used their claws and teeth to tear through the tape, while the mummies used their strength to do the rest. Under Einstein's supervision, the job was finished quickly. After the campers were freed, he instructed them to toss their ex-counselors into their own individual pods. "Have a nice trip, boys," Einstein said, "and don't bother to write."

"What happened to us?" Billy Armstrong shouted, looking at his paws. The rest of the werewolves looked at Einstein and howled for an answer.

"I can explain everything," Einstein said, "but we don't have much time."

The campers gathered around him in a circle.

"My fellow Creepy Timers," he began, "in less than twenty minutes a wormhole will open and we will all be sucked into outer space."

"Vat can ve do?" Vinnie asked.

"There is a time to fight and a time to run," Einstein replied.

"Mmmmm!" Manny and the rest of the mummies shouted.

"I agree with Manny! Let's run for our lives!" Einstein commanded, leading the way out into the corridor. He stopped and looked around. There was a small problem. He was lost. Greeley had transported him into the ship, but he had no clue how to get off. "Does anyone know how to get out of here?"

"I do," Roxie replied.

"Everyone follow Roxie," Einstein shouted. "Last one out of the spaceship is a rotten egg!"

CHAPTER

41

Day Eight — 2:22 P.M.

'll see you around the campfire, Fleet," Billy Armstrong said, holding out his paw. "I'm sorry for all the trouble."

Einstein knocked away the paw and gave him a bear hug. "Yeah, me too, Billy." The werewolf smiled, and then ran out of the barn, picking up a mummy along the way. Einstein shouted after him, "You guys still owe me a box of Twinkies!"

Roxie and Einstein watched the rest of the campers file out of the barn. The vampires turn into bats and flew away. The mummies moved slowly out the door, dragging strands of gauze and blue tape behind them. The werewolves picked them up, one by one, and carried them. Slowly, all the campers disappeared into the desert except for Einstein.

"It's time for you to go," Roxie whispered to Einstein. "Get as far away from the barn as you can. When the wormhole opens, everything within a fifty-yard radius of the barn will be sucked into deep space."

Einstein looked at Roxie and gave it one last shot. "You're sure that there is no other way?"

"I have a score to settle with Mucho Fahn," Roxie said firmly, "and nothing is going to stop me from settling it."

"Nothing?" Big Al said, standing behind them. Most of him had melted away. Other parts were still glowing blue and bubbling. "We'll see about that."

"That's impossible," Einstein said to Roxie, his voice shaking. "I liquidated him."

She shook her head. "You liquidated his disguise."

Big Al's entire body began to pulsate like a beating heart and what remained of his costume peeled away. A few small cracks of white light appeared, followed by a few more. Suddenly, Big Al exploded. All Einstein could see was his silhouette standing in the middle of a cloud of dust. The man was about six feet tall, but the alien was a good four feet taller and at least twice as broad. The sight sent shivers down Einstein's spine.

"It's time for Plan B!" he whispered to Roxie.

"We don't have a Plan B."

"Too bad." Einstein sighed. "We could really use one right about now."

Big Al stepped out of the cloud and glared at Einstein. He had eyes like a cobra. They were set into a crablike face with a large retractable jaw that exposed rows of small pointed fangs. His limbs were thick and muscular. They were covered with leathery layers of pale orange skin. The six fingers on each hand had nails as sharp as scalpels. In the middle of his tree trunk of a torso were two oversized bellies. Both were covered with rows of plates that jiggled when he spoke. "Say your prayers, chubby," Big Al bellowed at Einstein.

"Look who's talking," he whispered to Roxie. "He looks like he's ready to give birth to twins."

She grabbed Einstein's hand and ran. Big Al laughed at their attempt to escape, but didn't follow. As they reached the barn door and tried to pass through, they were stopped dead in their tracks, tumbling backward. Something hard and invisible was blocking their path. It was the force field.

"You're both trapped," Big Al roared.

"So are you," Roxie shouted back. "If we don't get in that spaceship, we're all going to die. When the wormhole opens, we will be sucked into space and torn to pieces."

Big Al seemed to find Roxie's observation amusing. "Either way we're dead," he replied as he started toward them. "Mucho Fahn will kill all of us as soon as we land. The only difference is I'm going to enjoy the look on your faces as I tear you limb from limb."

They literally had their backs up against the wall and there was nowhere to run. Big Al took his time as he approached, savoring every moment of fear. There wasn't much time left, but he didn't need much to do what he had in mind.

"HEY, BONEHEAD!"

Big Al turned around and saw Greeley standing behind him. "I brought you a playmate. I hear it's lonely up in space," the ghost said.

Godzilla roared at the alien. She circled him, looking for an advantage, and then charged. Big Al tried to fend her off, but he was clearly outmatched. He grabbed two of her eyes and pulled them off, which only seemed to infuriate the creature. She bit down on his arm and shook him like a rag doll. Big Al screamed in pain, but could not escape her viselike grip.

"Now that's something you don't see every day," Greeley said to Roxie. He smiled as Godzilla tossed Big Al across the barn. His head slammed against the spaceship with a loud thump. "Bet that's gonna leave a mark."

"I was wondering where you went," Einstein said.

"That big mutant spider was still alive," Greeley said. "I caught her chasing one of the campers and decided to kill two birds with one stone."

"So you brought her back here," Einstein said. "You know something, Greeley? You're pretty smart for an out-of-work mailman."

"You're not so bad yourself, Houdini."

"Oh, boys?" Roxie said, pointing at Einstein's wristwatch. "Could we finish this conversation somewhere else?"

Einstein took Greeley and Roxie by the hand and they formed a circle. "Beam us out of here, Scotty," he said, smiling at the ghost.

"Aye, Captain."

Big Al watched as the three of them disappeared. He was flat on his back, pinned beneath Godzilla. The female sank its fangs deep into his chest, mercifully injecting him with a powerful neurotoxin. Unable to move a muscle, he watched helplessly as the top of the roof of the barn disappeared and disintegrated before his eyes, revealing a dark, ominous funnel forming directly overhead. As the dark hole grew wider, bolts of lightning appeared, accompanied by loud claps of thunder. He stared into the eye of the wormhole and shuddered. It was a whirling dark black void extending into deep space, ominous and forbidding. As the barn itself was pulled farther and farther into the wormhole, everything began to spin. With each second, the rotation picked up speed, moving faster and faster. The walls of the barn began to melt as the rotation increased in velocity. "I really hate that kid," Big Al muttered to himself as his eardrums popped.

A moment later he was vaporized.

CHAPTER 42

Day Eight — 2:31 P.M.

They stood next to the police cruiser and stared slack-jawed at the dark sky, dumbfounded by a black funnel that had formed overhead. It had appeared suddenly and from out of nowhere, like a tornado. Claps of thunder were followed by huge streaks of lightning that could be seen for miles.

"What is that?" Shirley Fleet screamed.

"I don't know," Mr. Armstrong shouted, "but I'm gonna get my camera."

Suddenly, everything stopped and an eerie silence swept across the desert. The black swirling cloud disappeared and the funnel became completely transparent, like a long tube of glass. The tube reached into space for as far as the eye could see, like an escalator to the stars.

"You ever see anything like that before?" Norman asked the chief.

"Only on television," the stunned policeman replied.

As Armstrong began to snap pictures, an oblong silver disc shot through the tube and disappeared into space. Moments later, the skies cleared and the funnel was gone. "Ladies and gents, you're looking at the next cover for *The National Enquirer*,"

Armstrong said, showing the digital display on his camera to the group. "I just got me a picture of a genuine UFO."

The tears rolled down Norman's cheeks as he choked back a sob. Shirley hugged him and held him tight. "He's gone and it's all my fault," Norman whispered to his wife. "I'll never be able to forgive myself." They stood arm in arm staring at the empty sky, saying a silent prayer for their son.

"What are you looking at?" Einstein asked, standing behind them with Roxie at his side. After transporting them there, Greeley had promptly disappeared. Einstein would have enough explaining to do without adding a ghost to the mix. Camp Creepy Time would never be the same once word spread about what had happened. It wouldn't be another Roswell. It would be worse, especially for the campers.

"Einstein!" Shirley screamed, wrapping her arms around him. She squeezed Einstein so tight that he couldn't breathe.

"Mom, you're crushing me!"

"I don't care!" she sobbed. "I thought I'd never see you again."

Norman Fleet joined in on the hug. After they were done crushing him and messing up his hair, Einstein broke away and introduced them to Roxie. The Fleets exchanged a brief, but confused, look at each other. "The alien agent from PIMPS?" Norman Fleet said, giving his son the eye.

"IMPS," Einstein replied, correcting him. He looked at his father and smiled. "You didn't take all that stuff I wrote seriously, did you?"

Before Norman could answer, the chief walked up. "I'm Chief Chester of the Saugus Police Department," he said to Einstein. "Your parents have been worried sick about you. Heard a lot of talk about alien abduction, ghosts, and monsters. You want to tell me what's going on?"

Einstein wished he had never written the letters, but what was done was done. Now it was time to do some damage control. "The camp came down with some type of rare plague, I'm afraid," Einstein lied, "but everyone seems to be on the mend."

"Where are your counselors, young man?" the chief asked.

Einstein pointed to the sky. "Swept into space by the tornado."

"All of them?" Chief Chester asked.

"All of them except for Roxie," Einstein told the policeman.

"She looks a mite young to be a counselor," the chief said suspiciously.

"I'm in the counselor training program," Roxie replied, smiling at Einstein.

As Chief Chester prepared to continue his interrogation and get to the bottom of things, he was interrupted by the sound of cheering. He saw a group of campers hiking toward them. From a distance, they all seemed to be dressed in costumes. As they approached the police cruiser, Chief Chester rubbed his eyes to make sure that they weren't playing tricks on him. If the campers were on the mend as Einstein suggested, they still had a long way to go.

"It's my Billy!" Armstrong shouted.

"He-he's a werewolf," the chief stuttered.

"Yeah, isn't it great!" Armstrong replied. Sure, his son was a werewolf, but he didn't seem any worse for it. His acne was less noticeable beneath the facial hair and his foul temper seemed to have improved. All things being equal, Armstrong decided that he hadn't lost his boy; he'd gained a meal ticket.

One by one the rest of the campers showed up. There was a great deal of cheering and several high fives. The mummies lifted Einstein over their heads and paraded him around the police car. "Mmmmm!"

"You want to explain all this?" Norman Fleet shouted at his son.

"I thought I already did," Einstein replied.

"Hey, let's take a group photo!" Mr. Armstrong shouted. "Everyone gather around and smile at the birdie!"

"CAMP CREEPY TIME!" the campers shouted in unison.

"A genuine UFO and a camp filled with monsters!" he shouted as he snapped away with his camera. "This must be my lucky day!"

CHAPTER

43

Day Nine — 5:31 P.M.

The campers sat around a roaring fire, toasting marshmallows and singing songs. It was the last night at Camp Creepy Time and it called for a celebration. Einstein was smack-dab in the middle of it all, barbecuing hot dogs and burgers. He had gone from a sheltered introvert to the life of the party.

"Will you look at that," Norman said, nudging Shirley. "I don't believe it. Maybe Einstein was abducted after all and they left a clone in his place."

"I told you a little sunshine and fresh air wouldn't kill him," she replied.

Norman rolled his eyes and gave her a look.

"Well, he's not dead, is he?" his wife said in her own defense.

Einstein tried to keep up a cheerful facade, but it wasn't easy. Greeley's prediction had come to pass. Camp Creepy Time had become a regular Roswell. Within hours after the spaceship had passed through the wormhole, an army of FBI agents and men dressed in black suits had arrived with truckloads of high-tech equipment. They swarmed over every inch of the camp like ants, looking for clues as to what happened.

A team of doctors and scientists examined all of the campers, poking and prodding them to make sure that the "plague" was contained. The side effects of the illness seemed to have mysteriously reversed, but none of the medical experts had a clue as to why. The kids were promised that once they had received a clean bill of health from the government medics, they would be allowed to leave. Rather than trust the government with their fate, Einstein and the others had agreed to keep the antidote a secret. They divvied up the doses and kept their mouths shut. The feds could interrogate them and these quacks could examine them until they were blue in the face, but they wouldn't get the real story out of any of them and they couldn't keep them locked up at Creepy Time forever.

"How about a couple of burgers?" Vinnie said, bringing Einstein back into the moment. The little vampire had almost completed recovered, except for the two small fangs. He noticed that Einstein was staring. "If they don't go away, my father is going to file them down when we get home," he whispered.

Einstein reached into his pocket and secreted a black tablet into the center of the patty. "How would you like those bad boys?" he asked.

"Blood rare and mooing, of course."

Einstein spotted the Whammy sisters with their parents and another man, who looked like an attorney. Like the others who had been captured and cocooned by Godzilla, they were recovering the slowest. If it weren't for Greeley, they wouldn't have recovered at all. The old ghost had gone out to the desert and cut them loose, then administered a healthy dose of the antidote. Most of the campers seemed to be doing just fine except for the Whammy sisters. Apparently their witch noses looked just like their original hooked beaks and their parents were livid about having to cover the cost of two new nose jobs. They were threatening to sue. Einstein made a mental note to make sure that they got more of the antidote as soon as possible.

Billy Armstrong was standing next to his father, who was screaming bloody murder at a group of FBI agents. The fact that Billy's canines were still sharp and yellow didn't seem to bother Mr. Armstrong as much as the fact that they had confiscated his digital camera and his photos. The agents tried desperately to calm the man down and maneuvered to stay upwind from the argument. Billy bit one of the agents in the leg and had to be muzzled.

"Where is Roxie?" Vinnie asked as he slathered his hamburger bun with ketchup. "I haven't seen her all day."

Einstein had been wondering the same thing and he was worried. It was only a matter of time before they examined Roxie and discovered that they had a real live extraterrestrial on their hands. "Take over for me, will you, Vinnie?" Einstein asked, removing his apron and handing him the tongs. "I'm going to go find her."

Vinnie put on the apron and asked the next camper what he was having. Manny looked at the hamburger and pointed. "Mmmmm! That burger looks good!"

"Want a burger, mister?" Vinnie asked the next person in line.

The man, dressed in a conservative navy suit, shook his

head. "I'm looking for Einstein P. Fleet," he said. "Do you know where he is?"

"You just missed him," Vinnie replied, flipping a burger. He pointed at a couple standing about fifty yards away. "His parents are over there. Maybe they know."

The man walked up to the Fleets and introduced himself. "I'm not sure if you remember me," he said. "I'm Agent Smith with the FBI. I was the one who handled the Wilson case."

"We've apologized and paid the damages." Norman sighed. "Now what?"

"Relax, Mr. Fleet," the agent said. "As it turns out, your son had it right. Wilson *was* a deep cover agent. If it hadn't been for Einstein, we would have missed him altogether."

"You're kidding," Shirley said.

"I couldn't be more serious, Mrs. Fleet," the FBI agent replied. "On behalf of myself and a grateful nation, I'd like to thank you. Your son is a real hero."

"Does Einstein know about this?" Norman asked.

"Not yet," Agent Smith replied, "but I'm sure he won't be surprised. Knowing your son, he'll probably wonder what took us so long. Einstein is quite a character."

"Ain't that the truth?" Norman laughed. "Does this mean we get our money back?"

"What's going to happen to this place?" Shirley asked, ignoring her husband.

"That's up to Einstein," the agent replied. "The bureau was just informed that he bought the place a few minutes ago. In fact, that's why I wanted to speak with him."

"What are you talking about?" Norman groaned. "Einstein doesn't have any money."

Agent Smith couldn't help but laugh. Obviously, the Fleets didn't know their son quite as well as they thought they did. "We estimate that *The Smoking Peashooter* has over eight million active users. Each user pays ten dollars a year for membership. You do the math."

"You mean Einstein's a millionaire?" Shirley gasped.

"And then some, Mrs. Fleet," Smith replied. "Please tell him that I'd like to speak with him when you see him. We'd like to know what he intends to do with the camp." The agent said good-bye and walked away, leaving the Fleets standing there in a state of shock.

"I don't believe it," Shirley said to her husband. "No wonder Einstein didn't want to go away for eight weeks. He was running an empire from his room."

"And we thought he was crazy," Norman added.

"Poor people are crazy." Shirley laughed. "Rich people are eccentric."

"What's the difference?" he asked.

"Money."

CHAPTER

Day Nine — 6:10 P.M.

Einstein found Roxie sitting outside what was left of the caretaker's cottage. Her eyes were swollen and puffy. She saw Einstein and looked the other way.

"Is this your bunk assignment?" he asked, taking a seat beside her.

"That's on a need-to-know basis, Fleet," she replied without turning around, "and you don't need to know."

"Aren't you going to go to the farewell cookout?" he asked. "You're missing all the fun. It's a real circus down there."

"Cookouts are for weenies," she replied.

They sat together and watched the sunset. Slowly, the day turned into night and stars filled the sky. Einstein knew that she wasn't looking at the bright balls of light. Roxie was thinking about her brother, hoping that he was still alive and burning just as bright.

"You saved my life," she said. "I owe you one, Fleet."

"Now that you mention it," Einstein said, "you still owe me a buck. Are you planning on paying up or welshing on our bet?"

"Welshing," Roxie said. "If you want your money, you'll have to turn me in for the reward. I'll bet you could get more than a buck for a real live alien."

"Don't be so sure," Einstein said. "An alien that looks like a human is a tough sell. I could probably get more for Greeley."

"Where is he, anyhow? I haven't seen him all day."

"He went to check into something for me," Einstein replied, looking at his watch. "That old coot should have been back by now."

"Who you calling an old coot?" Greeley said, materializing beside him. The ghost handed a crumpled piece of notebook paper to Einstein and nodded.

"You're late, Greeley," he said, smiling.

"Take it out of my paycheck, Houdini," the ghost cackled.

"Well?" Einstein asked. "Did you find it?"

The ghost nodded.

"Excellent!" Einstein said, barely able to contain himself.

"Did you keep your end of the bargain?" Greeley asked.

"It's all ours, partner. We can break ground on the new camp as soon as we get back."

"What are you two talking about?" Roxie asked.

Einstein handed her the piece of paper. It contained a series of long numbers scribbled along the margin. "It's the coordinates for Mucho's monster zoo. I wasn't sure if it was possible for us to travel back through the wormhole, so I bribed Greeley to take a test flight. Let me tell you, the old ghoul drives a hard bargain. He insisted that I buy back the camp or no deal." He leaned over and whispered to Roxie, "Between you and me, I had nothing to lose. If Greeley didn't make it, I'd just back out of the deal."

"I heard that, sonny."

"Are you saying what I think you're saying?" Roxie gasped.

Einstein shook his head and smiled. "Care to take a ride via intergalactic g-mail, comrade?"

Roxie hugged Einstein so tight that his eyes crossed. She released him and he started to laugh.

"What's so funny, Fleet?" Roxie asked.

"I was just thinking about Bucky, Curly, and Nurse Knock-wurst," he replied. "Do you think they'll be happy to see us?"

"Let's go find out," Roxie replied.

They formed a circle and held hands with Greeley. The ghost looked at them and smiled. "Hold on tight," he warned. "It's going to be a bumpy ride."

"It always is, comrade," Einstein replied as they disappeared. "It always is."

EPILOGUE

One Month Later

The three moons of Gorza were peeking over the jagged ice-capped mountains, which were barely visible through the wispy patches of pink clouds that surrounded the peaks. It was unseasonably cold for this time of year, but not cold enough to keep anyone who was lucky enough to receive a private invitation to Mucho's Monster Zoo away. After all, it was a once-in-a-lifetime opportunity. Those who turned it down would never be invited again.

The guests were told where to meet at the last moment, blindfolded, and taken to a private spacecraft. As always, it was a top-secret event and the location was not disclosed. The trip cost them dearly, but was well worth the price of admission. Despite the fact that it was illegal to attend the zoo, it was considered an honor to be invited. Oddly enough, an invitation to the zoo was also considered the ultimate status symbol for the rich and ridiculously bored.

"Here they come," Curly announced to the others as a large crowd of tourists filed out of the spaceship. "Looks like Crotons."

"Crotons?" Bucky repeated, moving in for a closer look.

Despite having three heads, three plump rumps, and a rather hefty physique, the women of Croton were completely irresistible to Bucky. His eyes zeroed in on one of the females and his pulse soared. He pointed at the three protruding humps on her backside and elbowed Curly in the rib cage. "Check it out, my man. That is one fine-looking Croton mama."

Thirty days ago Curly wouldn't have given the Croton female a second look, but after the last month in the zoo, his standards had definitely been lowered. "You thinking what I'm thinking?"

"BOOTY CALL!" they yelled in unison. They slapped each other some skin.

"Triple the pleasure, triple your fun," Bucky said.

"You can say that again, brother!" Curly replied.

"You two are pigs!" Nurse Knockwurst growled.

"Not according to the sign," Curly reminded her. He pointed at a large black plaque with white block letters that was prominently displayed on their cage. "Can't you read?"

"Read this, you idiot!" The nurse punched Bucky in the nose and walked away. Big Al got off easy, she decided. The second they had materialized on the other side of the wormhole without the merchandise, Mucho Fahn had them thrown in a cage. He put them on exhibit as a reminder of what happened to those who failed to do his bidding. Although they were not one of the more interesting exhibits in the intergalactic monster zoo, they were certainly one of the most amusing. They were constantly bickering amongst themselves and calling one another names. Occasionally, the crowd was treated to a good old-fashioned fistfight. The best part of the day, however, was feeding time. Courtesy of Einstein, Mucho Fahn had been left the recipe for Twinkies, along with a note. Whatever the note said, Mucho must have found it amusing. He installed a vending machine right outside their cage and filled it with Twinkies. Above the machine, a flashing neon sign read **FEED THE MORONS**. It lit up like clockwork every hour on the hour, all day long.

Nurse Knockwurst noticed that Curly was ogling her. He had been doing it for days and it was getting on her nerves. "What are you staring at?" she growled.

"A whole lot of ugly," Curly replied.

Nurse Knockwurst pummeled him mercilessly with lefts and rights as a crowd gathered around the cage to watch the Morons go at it. She ripped off one of his eyebrows and tossed it to a member of the audience. The crowd cheered. While she was taking a bow, Curly jumped on her back and tried to pull her bun off. She bucked up and down like a bronco, trying to shake the cook loose. He was able to hold on for about ten seconds and then went sailing across the cell. The crowd went wild.

Suddenly, the light above the vending machine began to flash. "You clowns gotta chill," Bucky said, pulling them apart. "It's time for the two o'clock pelting."

They moved to the very back of the cage. It was feeding time.

"Who wants to feed the Morons?" a three-headed Croton asked his tribe of three-headed children. All sixteen of them raised their claws and began to squeal. They wagged their curly little tails with anticipation as their father dropped a few coins into the slot and the Twinkies began to flow. He distributed the golden brown treats equally amongst the kids. They made their way back to the cage and squeezed up to the front. The father pointed at Nurse Knockwurst. "That big ugly one looks really hungry. Go ahead, kids. Let's feed the Morons!"

The barrage of Twinkies began. Hundreds of golden projectiles were tossed into the cage, the cream-filled centers exploding upon impact. As always, Nurse Knockwurst seemed to take the brunt of the attack. Once feeding time was over, the crowd moved on to a new attraction. Those who missed the two o'clock feeding could always come back in an hour.

"This is all his fault," the nurse muttered as she wiped the goo from her face. With every Twinkie that was tossed in her face, her hatred for him grew stronger. One day she would have her revenge. She didn't know how or when, but she swore that somehow she would get even. Nurse Knockwurst raised a clenched fist at the sky and screamed loud enough for him to hear her millions of light-years away. "I'm going to get you, Einstein P. Fleet!" she bellowed. "I'll get you if it's the last thing I ever do!"